SUNSET RECKONING

Gunfighter Ed Blayney is recovering from bullet wounds when he is taken on as a cowhand by the CM Ranch. Any hopes of a quiet life are dashed when range war breaks out with a rival spread. To complicate matters further, Blayney falls in love with a beautiful Spanish immigrant who is coveted by ranch owner Christian Barrett. When Barrett sends his hired killers after Blayney, he finds himself having to face them as the sun sets on Chalmer's Hill.

SUNSET RECKONING

SUNSET RECKONING

by

Robert Eynon

Dales Large Print Books
Long Preston, North Yorkshire,
BD23 4ND, England.

British Library Cataloguing in Publication Data.

Eynon, Robert
    Sunset reckoning.

    A catalogue record of this book is
    available from the British Library

    ISBN   1-84262-405-9 pbk

First published in Great Britain 1993 by Robert Hale Limited

Copyright © Robert Eynon 1993

Cover illustration © Faba by arrangement with
Norma Editorial S.A.

Published in Large Print 2005 by arrangement with
Robert Hale Ltd.

Dales Large Print is an imprint of Library Magna Books Ltd.

Printed and bound in Great Britain by
T.J. (International) Ltd., Cornwall, PL28 8RW

Dedicated to
my friends at Caxton Press,
Treorchy

ONE

The bartender let the newspaper sag onto the gnarled wood of the counter when he heard the swing-doors open and close. He noted sadly that it was only a single customer to add to the trio already sitting at a table in the far corner of the room.

The newcomer was a stranger to the township. The bartender was confident in his assessment since the town of Milton boasted little over a hundred citizens, a rail-halt, a decrepit saloon, some thirty houses and shops and a small bank. It was fringed, however, by several acres of corrals to contain the thousands of head of cattle that arrived periodically at the end of the cattle drive.

The cattle and their drovers provided a welcome injection of wealth that kept this

Kansas outpost solvent throughout the lean months of the year. They also caused an influx of ladies known as 'soiled doves' who left their winter quarters in St Louis and Memphis and came to fill the busy beds of Milton's whorehouse that stood conveniently right next door to the above mentioned Bank of Commerce.

'I'll have a beer,' the stranger said quietly when the bartender had sauntered over from the far end of the counter.

'Any particular kind?' the barman enquired with a touch of pride that there should be any choice at all.

'The cheapest,' the stranger replied frankly and without embarrassment.

He was a man in his late twenties, over average height and slight of build. His fair hair was bleached by the sun and his face tanned, but there was a pallor lurking beneath the surface of the skin. His cheeks were pinched, too, as if he'd been down on his luck for a while, or sick maybe.

The bartender poured the beer lovingly

from a wooden barrel behind the counter, then handed it over without spilling a drop. The stranger eyed it thoughtfully for a moment, then glanced at the three men seated in the corner of the room. They'd had a good look at him when he came in, but by now they'd lost interest in him. Nevertheless, his arrival seemed to stir them out of their lethargy. One of them turned to his companions and muttered.

'He ain't coming in tonight. We may as well take a walk.'

The three of them rose to their feet and began to wend their way through the tables and chairs. The eldest looked a typical gambler. His velvet jacket was adorned by a gleaming badge that might have a military significance or point to his membership of a club or society back east. The two men with him were dressed much more casually; they were obviously townsfolk since they wore none of the accoutrements of a range-rider.

They passed the stranger without a glance as they made for the door and walked out into the dusk.

'Unless things pick up,' the bartender remarked suddenly, 'I'll be closing early tonight.'

The stranger shrugged his shoulders; his pockets weren't full enough to keep a saloon open.

'Strange thing is,' the bartender confided, 'it's been real busy for weeks. You probably noticed there's still steers in the corrals.'

His solitary customer nodded his head and sipped his beer.

'Trouble is, two ranches from the same part of Colorado drove cattle in a few days ago – that's the Shallow Creek outfit and the CM spread.'

He couldn't tell from the stranger's face whether he was interested or not, so he decided to continue the tale regardless.

'Them two bunches of boys get on like scorpions and tarantulas,' he said. 'For a few nights they just about tolerated each other, then last night there was a fight that started outside the whorehouse and ended up outside this saloon.'

'But not inside?' the stranger inquired between sips of beer.

'Nope. As good luck had it the two fellers who run the CM ranch were in here drinking. One of them went onto the verandah and told his men to get out of town, and pronto.'

'And they did?'

'Yip, and it looks like they ain't coming in tonight either,' the bartender added regretfully. 'As for the Shallow Creek hands, they finished loading up today and I guess they've high-tailed it home already.'

'Sounds like they've got a good boss at the CM ranch,' the stranger observed.

The bartender grinned.

'I loaned him my shotgun to go outside,' he admitted cheerfully. 'In case the other bunch didn't take telling from him. When you got lots of crazy cowboys in town and no lawman you cain't take no chances.'

'You said there were two bosses from the CM spread in the saloon,' the stranger reminded him. 'What did the other one do?'

'Oh, him...' the bartender pulled a face. 'I don't reckon he's up to much; he ain't half the man his brother is. He just went on gambling with those fellers you just saw going out. He didn't want no part of the trouble outside. He had plenty on his mind in here, I reckon. He lost more money than he was carrying on him. Said he'd be in to pay it back tonight. Reckon that's why them hombres are so restless...'

TWO

Christian Barrett rode into Milton towards dusk and was surprised to find it nearly deserted. The young rancher's head still ached from the liquor he'd put away the night before.

Apart from the headache and queasy

stomach, Barrett was angry to have to come into town to pay a debt. Last night he'd overplayed his luck in the saloon and ended up owing over a hundred dollars to a couple of nobodies and a card-sharping dude called Schneck.

It wasn't that Barrett believed in honouring debts; the problem was that the CM outfit still had to load longhorns onto cattle-wagons over the next few days. If Schneck and his two cronies branded him a welcher it would spread around the plains like wildfire.

He noticed some empty corrals at the side of the railroad. The Shallow Creek steers were on their way to the east. There was no sign of their drovers, none of the usual revelry and high-spirits that announced the end of the cattle-drive. He smirked to himself; the Shallow Creek hands must have taken a real beating the previous night if they were afraid to hang around the township for their final fling.

His feeling of satisfaction was only fleeting. While his brother Marcus had braved both factions and put a stop to the fighting, Christian had been stupidly losing a cool hundred to a bunch of double-dealers.

He spotted the red lamp glowing above the doorway next to the bank. The whorehouse was a pleasure he'd not indulged in during his stay. His position as co-owner of the CM spread prevented him from indulging in some of the pleasures of a common cowboy.

He pulled the horse over to the right. As he approached the building he imagined he could smell the perfumed flesh of soiled doves inside. The town was so quiet now, and he knew that the CM ranch hands were confined to camp on his brother's orders because of the trouble the previous night.

He dismounted and tied his horse to a convenient rail halfway between the whorehouse and the Bank of Commerce. As if by design the door beneath the red light swung open and a blonde girl stood staring at him with vacant eyes. The girl's dress fell away from her shoulders and her pale skin reflected the red glow, making her body look warm and inviting.

Christian Barrett, still in his early twenties, had no particular weakness; they were legion and usually latched onto the nearest available temptation – the blonde girl in this instance.

'You busy,' he inquired, his voice croaky with excitement.

The girl giggled and shook her head.

'None of us is busy, mister,' she admitted. 'You coming in?'

He woke up from his deep sleep with a blinding headache. As he turned over in the bed his arm brushed up against a girl's naked body. Shit, he thought, what number was she – the fourth, the fifth?

He could remember sending the fat madame out for whiskey, lots of the stuff. She'd made more than one trip to the saloon while he'd satiated his desires between the sweaty sheets of the girls' beds. His throat was so dry it hurt to swallow. He lay on his back as the room took a couple of turns before returning to normal.

Suddenly he heard a man's voice at the bottom of the stairs. It was a familiar voice, but for a moment he couldn't place it. Then the image of the card game came back to him and sent a violent nervous pain through his head.

He threw the sheet to one side and lurched out of the bed. He had to lean on the wall to steady himself. God, was he drunk! He could hear a woman's voice now, protesting something about invasion of privacy. He had to get out of the place before they found him, but how could he find his clothes in this goddam darkness?

Someone heavy was coming up the stairs. Then the door burst open and light flooded in from the passageway revealing his nakedness and that of the girl on the bed.

'Stop that!'

A strong hand curled around his wrist.

Instinctively he'd reached for his gunbelt, but now it was wrenched away from him. He blinked to cope with the light but they were all shadows to him.

'You no causa trouble,' the madame admonished from the staircase. 'You no harma the girlies.'

Fingers were pressing into the side of his neck.

'Get your pants on, Barrett.'

The madame was still squealing shrilly.

'You make me trouble, Mr Schneck, and you getta no more girlies. You hear?'

Barrett struggled into his pants. As he straightened up someone pushed the rest of his clothes into his arms.

'You got the money you owe us?' Schneck demanded from the doorway. He'd leave the rough stuff to his two companions.

'Sure,' Barrett said thickly. 'I got it.'

'Bring all his stuff,' the gambler said.

The young rancher found himself propelled down the stairs and out into the street. The fat madame had to press herself into a recess as the men passed by.

'You go far away,' she called out to them. 'This house gotta good name to keep.'

They walked past Christian Barrett's horse that wore the CM brand prominently on its flank. Barrett realized ruefully how they'd found him so easily.

'In here,' Schneck said suddenly, and Barrett was pushed into a dark alleyway at the side of the bank. 'Now let's see your money, boy.'

'Sure, sure.'

He searched in his pants pockets, then his shirt and jacket pockets with increasing panic.

'I had well over a hundred dollars.' he told them plaintively. 'She's robbed me, the goddam bitch!'

A punch to the pit of his stomach doubled him up and made him retch on the spot. Another blow to the side of the head knocked him off his feet and onto the hard ground. As they began kicking him he instinctively rolled into a ball. All the time the tears were flooding from his eyes and his cracked lips pleaded for mercy and a chance to pay them what they were owed.

THREE

The stranger was well within the glow of the camp-fire before he was challenged. A cowboy emerged from the shadow of a waggon, carrying a loaded carbine in his hands.

'You got business here, mister?' he inquired.

The stranger halted and nodded his head in the direction of the horse he was leading. There was a man lying across its saddle.

'Could be,' he replied laconically. 'That's for you to decide.'

The cowboy moved warily to the side of the horse, placed his hand on the scalp of the inert rider and jerked his head to one side so that he could see his face.

'Jeez,' he gasped. 'It's Christian Barrett!'

He let the head drop gently back and turned towards the camp fire.

'Mr Barrett ... Mr Barrett!'

Cowhands rolled out of their blankets and sleeping-bags, and staggered to their feet. Each of them reached instinctively for his gunbelt at the first sign of trouble. Any place outside the ranch was potentially hostile territory to a cattle drover.

A short, sturdy youth led the way. When he saw that the newcomer was covered by his sentry's carbine he sheathed his Colt, though the men around him did not follow suit.

'Who are you?' he asked. His tone was business-like, but not hostile. He looked very young to be in charge of a show like this, not much over twenty. However, he looked resolute and in command and his gaze was penetrating.

'My name's Blayney – Ed Blayney,' the stranger informed him.

'That's Christian on the horse,' the man

with the carbine blurted out. 'He's hurt pretty bad.'

The blood drained from Barrett's face.

'Get him over to the fire,' he ordered. 'Where's Crocker?'

A huge figure loomed out of the fire's glow.

'Here I am, Marcus.'

'Christian's hurt bad,' Barrett told him. 'See what you can do for him. If you need a doc, I'll ride all night for one.'

Some of the cowboys went over to the horse and lifted Christian Barrett gingerly from its back. As they carried him towards the fire others crowded them in their curiosity to see the nature of the wounds.

'Give him air, damn you,' Crocker bawled. 'And git out of our way.'

Marcus Barrett didn't seem to have the stomach to look too closely at his stricken brother for the moment. He stood there facing Blayney as three shadowy figures moved nonchalantly into position round them.

Even in this poor light Blayney could tell them for what they were – hired guns. They'd been there all the time, he guessed, but unobtrusive, waiting for the moment their skills were needed. Now they were hovering around the man who paid them, like hornets around a pot of jam.

'What happened to him?' Marcus Barrett demanded.

'I don't know.'

The answer was honest as far as it went, but Blayney had already put two and two together. He'd seen three men emerge from the alleyway as he was making his way along the main street after leaving the saloon. He couldn't fail to recognize the gambler and his companions whom he'd seen drinking earlier in the evening.

He'd heard the laboured breathing as he passed the bank. Instead of minding his own business as common sense indicated, he'd stepped into the darkness and stumbled across the battered body of the young rancher.

'You'd better be telling the truth, mister,' one of the gunslingers warned him suddenly.

Blayney ignored the remark.

'Take a look at the mare, Mr Barrett,' he suggested. 'Is it one of yours?'

Barrett didn't need to get any closer.

'It's my brother's horse,' he said. 'Why d'you ask?'

'If it didn't belong to your brother I'd have to take it back, that's why,' Blayney pointed out. 'I don't want to swing for horse theft.'

For the first time the rancher seemed to realize the risk the stranger had taken to bring his brother back to the safety of the camp. Whoever had done this to Christian must hate him pretty bad. They might well feel the same way about anyone who tried to help him.

'I'm sorry,' Marcus Barrett said. 'You've been the good samaritan and I've been treating you like an enemy.'

He turned to the nearest gunslinger.

'Jensen,' he said. 'Get this feller some coffee and some chow. I'll go see how my brother's getting on.'

He turned again to face Blayney.

'D'you live in town?' he asked.

'Nope. I'm on the move.' Blayney replied.

'You got a place to stay tonight?'

The cowboy shook his head.

'No place in particular.'

'Where's your horse?'

'Ain't got one,' Blayney admitted with a hint of regret in his voice.

'Cain't expect you to walk all the way back to town,' the young rancher mused aloud. 'You can stay here tonight. The boys will get you a bed-roll. We'll work things out in the morning.'

FOUR

The next morning found Christian Barrett suffering as much from the hangover as from the injuries inflicted by his three attackers. He acknowledged his brother Marcus' concern rather grumpily and avoided giving a straight answer about what had happened the night before.

'I just got jumped, that's all,' he muttered. 'They must have been waiting for me in the alley. Nope, I didn't get a good look at them. It was too dark. I guess they was just drifters off one of the trains.'

However, he did acknowledge that he'd been robbed.

'Money ain't what's important,' his brother consoled him. 'You could have got yourself killed. I'm sorry now that I kept the rest of the boys in camp; if they'd been with you nothing would have happened.'

Christian Barrett merely glared at him. Marcus was a simpleton, but there was no denying that it was Marcus that the men respected, despite the fact that Christian was the elder by one year. Christian was sure that the cowhands would be sniggering at his latest misadventure. They doubted his courage and were only fearful of his deviousness and animal cunning. Christian Barrett had an easy smile when he wanted a favour; but when crossed he was vindictive and vengeful.

Strangely, Marcus Barrett was blind to his brother's defects, or at least he excused them in a charitable fashion. But instead of reciprocating his kindness, Christian resented it; Marcus' good-nature was mere stupidity in his eyes and he disparaged his brother's qualities of leadership, though secretly he yearned to be boss man on the ranch if he'd had the guts for the job.

Crocker, the camp cook and also its provisional doctor, assured Marcus that all his brother's wounds would heal in time, with a little help from Crocker's famed herbal remedies. When Marcus had thanked him for his work during the night Crocker brought up the subject of the cowboy who'd brought Christian Barrett into camp.

'I got him stirring the gruel back at the chuck-waggon,' Crocker said.

The rancher smiled at him; the good news about his brother made him feel better.

'Let's go see how he's getting on,' he suggested. 'I'm feeling peckish myself.'

They walked over to the covered waggon. Ed Blayney let go of the ladle and straightened up as they approached.

'I didn't thank you properly last night, Blayney,' Barrett said, taking the cowboy's hand in a firm grip. 'Now that Christian's over the worst, I guess I'm thinking clearly again.'

'You thanked me enough by feeding me last night,' Blayney acknowledged frankly, his fair hair glinting in the morning sun.

Barrett and Crocker exchanged glances.

'I reckon he could do with more than just one meal, Marcus,' the big man ventured. 'The heaviest thing about him is his .45. Anyways, so far he's helped out to pay for the hospitality.'

Barrett heeded the cook's remark and scrutinized the newcomer closely. Blayney's shirt hung loosely on his shoulders and his belt was pulled in tight. He guessed that somewhere along the line the cowboy had lost a stone or more in weight, and he didn't look any the healthier for it.

'You heading any place, Blayney?' the young rancher asked.

The cowboy shrugged his shoulders, and Barrett turned to address Crocker.

'Could you do with some extra help?' he inquired.

'There's always work to do,' the cook pointed out.

Barrett nodded thoughtfully. Several of his drovers had merely come along for the ride. Once back home they'd tire of the mono-tony of the range and go seeking the excitement of the town where casual work was plentiful.

'D'you fancy giving it a try?' he asked Blayney.

'I'll try anything, Mr Barrett,' the cowboy told him. 'Thanks.'

His first day was more hectic than he expected. To introduce him to the rest of the drovers, Marcus Barrett included him in the detail assigned to loading the penned cattle onto the railway waggons.

So it was that Ed Blayney took his place near the track and heard the whistle of the approaching goods train. Following the example of his fellow herders he used a long pronged rod to urge the cattle from the pen up the narrow ramp and into the darkness of the waggons. When each waggon was full to bursting with lowing steers he helped slide the bars across the heavy doors to secure them for the long journey. When the train finally pulled away from the halt he trudged with his companions to Milton's lone saloon and slaked his thirst with tepid beer that tasted like nectar to his parched palate.

In the saloon he caught sight of the gambler again. Schneck was not playing at this early hour, but Blayney could see that the gambler kept a vigilant eye on the assembled cowboys in case word had got round of his involvement in the beating outside the whorehouse.

As it was, no word had got around. Even if it had, Shneck struck Blayney as a man who could look after himself if it came to gunplay. For all their swaggering and willingness to fire a gun in the air during a spree, most cattle drovers were ordinary fellers just eking out a living for themselves.

Men like Schneck, on the other hand, used their speed of hand to avoid hard work, and a gambler's hand sometimes needed to deal him a Colt from his holster or a derringer from his sleeve as quickly as an ace or a picture card from the bottom of the pack.

A man like Shneck did not believe he was invincible, but he could confidently expect to take two or three men to hell with him if he lost his life in a saloon shoot-out.

The drinking was not overdone on his occasion since the cowboys realized that there'd be more hard work under a fierce sun the following day. When they finally retired to camp Crocker, the cook, noted the fatigue and pallor in Ed Blayney's face. It was going to take time, and good food, to bring the cowboy back to full health after whatever illness had assailed him.

FIVE

If Ed Blayney found the next few days too hectic and exhausting to think, the same could not be said for Christian Barrett. The young rancher avoided the township of Milton like the plague. Instead he moped around the campsite all day long, still feeling the painful effects of the beating he'd taken to the head and ribs.

More irksome than the physical discomfort, however, was the smarting memory of the way his dignity had been humbled by a card-sharp and a pair of smalltime hicks. His resentment festered inside his guts until it stopped him sleeping at night, in spite of the liberal swigs of whiskey he took from the bottles his brother thoughtfully provided him with.

His only companions in this sullen brooding were the three gunslingers, Jensen, Young and Pope. These men rarely mixed with the rest of the cowhands, and certainly were not called upon to soil or chafe their hands with the hard work of the cattle-drive. Their job was to ride along as trouble-shooters and deal with any problems, whether from rival cattle outfits or from the Indians along the trail who'd use any method to exact a toll from the herds passing through their lands. If this toll wasn't exacted in money they'd settle for a few head of cattle, either known or unknown to the ranchers.

Jensen, Pope and Young were good at their job – too good sometimes. Along the trail Marcus had had to keep them on a tight rein, especially when Indians showed up. It was customary for the trail boss to compromise with Indians' demands, but the gunslingers' idea of compromise was to greet the redskins' demands with a hail of bullets and worry about the consequences later.

Since his brother's beating Marcus had ordered the three gunslingers to stick close to him. Christian's silence about the incident made it seem all the more mysterious to Marcus, and he didn't want Christian's attackers to pay a surprise visit to the campsite and dole out further punishment.

Two days went by before Christian Barrett confided to Jensen and the others an account of what had befallen him in the alleyway between the bank and the whorehouse where he'd spent the money he owed from his cardplay in the saloon.

The three hired guns listened to his story with unblinking eyes. Christian Barrett was so full of his own woes that he failed to see how childish his whining appeared to his audience. When he'd finished pouring his heart out to them, Jensen put one single question to him.

'Do you want us to handle it for you?'

The young rancher gulped. He'd expected to have to work hard on these men who'd always shown more respect for his brother than for him. Before he could reply Pope broke in with a question of his own.

'You sure the two fellers with the gambler work in a sawmill, Mr Barrett?'

Christian nodded his head.

'They talked about getting a load of logs in on the train,' he said. 'They take them the rest of the way by waggon.'

'The sawmill will be down by the river,' Jensen mused. 'The gambler will be easy to find.'

'What about the law?' Young inquired casually, but without too much concern in his voice.

'There ain't no lawman in town,' Christian

Barrett said eagerly. 'It's only a one-horse place.'

The gunslingers were not so well acquainted with the town. They'd drifted in one afternoon for a quick drink, but they'd not divulged to anyone that they were hired by the CM spread. Marcus Barrett had discouraged them from doing any evening drinking when the rival hands of the Shallow Creek ranch were in town. Their presence among a carousing group of cowhands would have been provocative and more likely to cause trouble than prevent it.

'We'd best not do anything till our boys have finished loading,' Young warned. 'That way nobody will connect us to this outfit.'

Jensen scratched his chin thoughtfully.

'Trouble is,' he pointed out, 'our contract ends at the end of the trail.'

His meaning did not escape the young rancher.

'I ... I'll square things with Marcus,' he told them after a moment's hesitation. 'I'll tell him we'll need fellers like you when we get back to the ranch.'

Jensen's eyes were boring into Christian's face as he spoke, and the young rancher felt a chill go through his body.

'You do that, Mr Barrett,' the gunslinger advised him. 'We'll be depending on you.'

When the last of the cattle were duly loaded onto the eastbound train, the CM ranch hands enjoyed one final night of carousing in Milton before embarking on the long ride home to South Colorado.

Christian Barrett did not join them and neither did the three gunslingers, Jensen, Pope and Young. Christian Barrett took it upon himself to settle the wage bill they'd earned for their escort duties. Normally it was Marcus who attended to such things but the easy-going rancher acceded to Christian's request without question. In fact Marcus Barrett was pleased to see his elder brother take an interest in what was going on. There was not much work in Christian and sometimes it was a heavy burden that

Marcus bore to keep the ranch running smoothly.

In spite of their heavy heads the ranch hands rose early the next morning as was their custom. There was an air of excitement as they saddled their mounts and loaded their excess equipment onto the chuck waggon. They were on their way home to family and friends with money in their pockets; the lean days were over for a while at least.

Nobody even bothered to take their leave of the three gunslingers, who were still seated around the embers of the fire when the CM drovers departed westwards.

The day was off to a warm and sunny start and Jensen, Pope and Young were in no hurry to leave the site. It was still quite early morning and they didn't expect Shneck the gambler to be quick off the mark after a late night in the saloon. As for the sawyers, they'd be up early but they'd be easy to locate at the mill.

The three men sat smoking until the fire finally died and yielded up its last strands of black smoke to the blue sky. Then Jensen rose to his feet and walked over to his horse.

'I'll take the gambler,' he informed his companions, 'You can head for the sawmill.'

'What about later?' Young asked. 'We meeting up again today?'

'Reckon so,' Jensen replied. 'I'll ride up river. First fork I come to I'll wait for you. You do the same.'

Young nodded his head. There was no point in them splitting up too long; Milton was unlikely to be able to summon a posse to pursue them, and even if there was a pursuit he was confident they'd be able to handle it if they stuck together.

As Jensen made his way casually in the direction of the township. Pope and Young followed the sloping terrain down towards the river that ran in a deep gully that swept around Milton from the north to the east. As they rode they made a final check of their Colts to ensure that no dust had got into them in the night and that the magazine cylinders rotated smoothly.

They were guided to the gully by the sound of the river that was flowing quite strongly with cold water from the snowclad summits away to the west. Within a short time they were guided more accurately by the creaking of the water-wheel of the sawmill and the intermittent whine of the saw that it drove inside the mill.

The sawyers had dammed the river upstream of the mill. It was the force of the water issuing from the dam that drove the wheel and gave the saw its power. The mill was built into the side of the gully with windows opening out onto the river and a roadway cut down the hillside to allow waggons access to the sawmill.

The two gunslingers dismounted at a point above the mill and continued their way on foot. Young noticed that a single-track pathway skirted the river and passed under the wall of the sawmill.

'You drop down to the river bank,' he told Pope. 'I'll just walk in.'

Pope had got the picture. From the

pathway it would be easy to dominate the windows of the mill and also the interior if he could get that close.

Young waited for him to drop out of sight, before walking boldly into the yard of the mill. For a moment he thought that it was deserted, then a few logs tumbled over to his left and made him start.

'Them dam' logs, they don't never stay where you put them,' a voice grumbled.

A bent figure emerged from the piles of debris that littered the untidy yard. The man was old and not at all nimble. When he spotted Young staring at him the old man's jaw sagged stupidly. The gunslinger wondered if he'd have the intelligence to answer any questions.

'Where's the boss?' he asked brusquely.

The old man didn't even have to think about it.

'They're both inside,' he said. 'Cain't you hear them?'

The saw was in fact rotating busily. Young ignored the remark.

'You got a lot of men working here?' he inquired.

'Why?' the old man demanded. 'You looking for work?"

'Maybe.'

'Well, you won't find none here,' the old feller snapped possessively. 'Dill and Laz does all the cutting and carrying, and I do all the sweeping up.'

He'd told the visitor straight and he turned his back on him to show that the conversation was over. He suddenly remembered the logs that had fallen out of place and he shuffled over to where they lay. He never got there.

Young took a few quick steps forward, drawing his gun as he moved. He brought it down with a thud on the back of the old man's head. The old feller gave a sort of sigh and crumpled forward onto the sawdust-strewn ground.

Without bothering to check if the man was alive or dead, Young took up position at the edge of the open door. He peered into the interior and allowed his eyes to adjust to the comparative gloom of the mill before venturing any further.

Just one of the two sawyers was visible to him. The man's body was crouched over a log that he was feeding into the rotating blade amidst a cloud of dust. Young approached cautiously, his eyes darting left and right as he moved in case the other man was lying in wait for him.

He raised his Colt to eye level and held it in both hands. As the gun exploded the sawyer jerked upright momentarily. The second slug knocked him forward against the sawblade which cut into his upper arm, splashing blood onto his face, then hurled him away onto the floor like a rag doll.

Young retreated into the shadows.

'Dill...' The voice betrayed a mixture of shock and fear. Young judged it to come from a far corner of the workshop. 'Dill...!'

The gunslinger broke his six-gun open and replaced the two spent cartridges. A moment or two passed in silence and he wondered what Pope was up to outside.

Suddenly a figure lurched into the middle of the room. As Young jerked his gun up a shotgun shattered the silence and the wall behind him pounded. Young leapt desperately to one side before the sawyer could aim the second barrel.

As he ran his foot struck a log on the floor and he went flying. The accident probably saved his life as the next shotgun blast blew a hole in the wooden rampart above him. Then he heard shots from a six-shooter. He looked up and saw the sawyer stagger as one of Pope's slugs entered his ribs. Young raised his Colt as well and fired a shot into the man's stomach.

The sawyer dropped to his knees and then fell forward onto his face. A shadow crossed the floor as Pope clambered in through the open window.

Young climbed to his feet and limped across to where the body lay.

'The sonofabitch' he grumbled to Pope. 'He made me tear my breeches!'

45

The bartender didn't like the look of Jensen from the moment he came into the empty saloon. He figured he'd seen him before but couldn't relate him to any particular outfit.

'Give me a whisky,' Jensen ordered him. 'And make it a good one.'

The bartender ignored the bottles on the shelf behind him. Instead, he reached under the counter and got out a bottle without a label.

'This is good,' he assured his surly customer. 'I drink it myself.'

Jensen knocked it back without comment and pushed the glass forward for a refill.

'You always this busy?' he inquired drily.

'Drovers been and gone,' the bartender replied equably. 'There'll be a few of the local folk in later.'

Jensen sipped the second drink with more respect.

'I was hoping for a game of cards,' he said.

The bartender looked up at the clock.

'Mr Schneck will be in dead on noon,' he

replied. 'He'll take anyone on at blackjack.'

'Is that what he does for a living, playing cards?' Jensen asked.

'Yip, nothing else. Once he's through having his shave and trim he'll be straight along.'

The gunslinger noted that it was barely eleven-thirty. He downed his drink and walked over to the door without a word.

The barber's pole was attached to the façade of Milton's saddler's store. Jensen walked straight in and saw an empty chair standing in the middle of the floor amongst all the horse-tack and leather work. There was nobody behind the counter, so he slammed the door noisily behind him and went and sat in the empty chair.

Within a few seconds a plump, oily-skinned man came through a side door carrying a steaming bowl of water and a white cloth over his arm.

'I'm told I can get a shave here,' the gunslinger said, running his hand over the stubble on his chin.

'Shave's fifty cents,' the shopkeeper informed him. 'Only I got another customer coming in any minute now.'

'That's okay,' Jensen grinned crookedly. 'This stubble won't take long.'

He tossed a dollar onto the counter and relaxed in the chair. The barber hesitated for a moment, then decided to take the easy way out. He wrapped the white cloth around the gunslinger's shoulders and chest and went to look for his razor.

The shave was halfway through when Schneck the gambler came into the shop. He looked none too pleased to see the chair already occupied.

'I won't be long, Mr Schneck,' the barber apologized. 'Grab a chair.'

The gambler declined the offer and went and stood at the counter, drumming his fingers irritably on the woodwork.

Every thirty seconds he pointedly took out his gold pocket-watch and examined it as if half an hour had gone by. Meanwhile Jensen just stared straight ahead as if unaware that anything was wrong.

'Reckon that's about it, mister,' the barber declared at last.

Schneck muttered something inaudible under his breath and stopped tapping the counter.

'I don't know,' Jensen drawled lazily. 'Maybe you should take the moustache clean off as well.'

By now the gambler had had enough. He came over to the chair and towered above the seated gunslinger.

'Look here, mister,' he yelled red-faced. 'If you don't get the hell...'

Jensen fired into his body through the white cloth. Schneck's eyes opened wide then he jack-knifed and keeled over sideways onto the floor.

Jensen had whipped the cloth off his body, but his Colt was still unsheathed. The barber watched the blood and life drain out of Schneck's body through the hole in his silk waistcoat. He didn't dare make a movement to help him.

When the gambler finally stopped twitching, Jensen replaced the gun in its holster.

'I gave you a dollar just now,' he reminded the barber. 'That should cover the cloth as well.'

SIX

Ed Blayney travelled the trail back to Colorado at the side of the big man, Crocker. The CM outfit had broken up as an entity as small groups of men made their own way back at their own pace. Since Crocker was the man who'd been closest to him during the few days at Milton, Blayney turned down the offer to ride ahead with the ranchers themselves.

'If it's okay with you I'll stick with the chuck-waggon,' he told Marcus Barrett. 'I ain't in no hurry.'

Barrett was happy to assent. Blayney

would be company for the camp cook. Despite his youth Marcus Barrett had worked alongside many men, and he'd already summed Blayney up as dependable and loyal. Not that the newcomer had said much about himself; he was on the quiet side, but not taciturn.

Barrett could tell that Blayney was not a cowpoke by profession; the few days work at the railroad corrals had plumb tuckered the feller up. What Barrett liked was the way Blayney had stuck to the job without complaining and without being a burden on the other cowhands.

The young rancher guessed that the stranger's strength might lie in the pearl-handled Colt in his gunbelt, but he couldn't even be sure of that since Blayney lacked the swagger and self-confidence of the gun-slingers, Jensen, Pope and Young, nor did he share their disdain of the ordinary cowboys and the work they did.

So it was that Ed Blayney travelled and slept in the covered chuck waggon, occasion-

51

ally taking over the reins from Crocker, but more often not since the cook was a man who liked to keep busy at all times.

Crocker was open and talkative for a frontiersman. There was French blood somewhere in his ancestry and it gave him an excitable side to his character and a desire to communicate through word and gesture. For all his size and strength Crocker was a gentle man who preferred reasoning to quarrelling and who would go out of his way to help a fellow human being.

As the waggon rolled leisurely westwards the cook filled his passenger in about the CM spread and the surrounding ranches.

'It ain't a big spread,' he said. 'Least, not like some of the ranches I've worked on down Texas way. Then again, it ain't so small when you've got to round up the mavericks. The pasture's pretty good and there's a river that's never been known to run dry even in drought.'

He put his left hand down and touched the wooden seat as he spoke. Drought was a plague in parts of the west.

'Far side of the river the land rises pretty steep,' he said. 'It ain't cattle country, but the ravines feed the main river when it rains, then dry up with the summer. It's good hunting country all year round.'

'What about Shallow Creek ranch?' Blayney inquired, since he'd heard of rivalry between the two outfits.

'That's upriver from us,' Crocker informed him. 'Then there's the Garieta place; that's further upstream again.'

'Garieta? They Mexican?'

Crocker grinned and flicked the rein to remind the horses they were expected to keep a steady pace.

'I'd say so,' he said. 'But old man Garieta reckons they're Spaniards of pure blood and that they came in this country through New York, not Vera Cruz. *Sangre castiza* he calls it, or something like that.'

'What's the trouble between the CM ranch and the Shallow Creek?' Blayney asked.

The cook shrugged his shoulders.

'Nothing much,' he replied. 'It blew up out of nothing after the cholera.'

He stopped speaking for a moment to lick the gummed edge of his cigarette paper.

'The cholera got Mr Barrett senior and his good lady,' he went on. 'That was four years back. It didn't touch Marcus and Christian, nor their sister Katy.' He shook his head sadly at the memory. 'They were still kids,' he said. 'It hit them pretty hard. Still, they pulled through with a little help from friends and a few old hands like me.'

His voice had a touch of pride as he recollected the struggle.

'What about the Shallow Creek ranch?' Blayney persisted.

'They weren't touched by cholera,' Crocker explained. 'Leastways, not the family. 'Course, old man Kemp died years ago. Ma Kemp ran the place single-handed for years, till Matthew was old enough to take over. They got cowhands, too, almost as many as our spread.'

He lit his smoke and savoured it.

'Christian Barrett and Matthew Kemp are the same age,' he said. 'They don't get on – never did. Don't ask me why, I ain't never figured it out. It was worse after the cholera, like as if Christian resented the way it hit the Barretts and left the Kemps alone.' He glanced across at his companion. 'Guess that's how some folks think,' he observed.

'If both spreads have access to water,' Blayney commented, 'I don't see any reason for a clash.'

'That's because you ain't Christian Barrett,' Crocker said. 'You see, Christian don't like the idea of being downstream from Shallow Creek land. He's forever sending men onto Kemp territory to check that they ain't diverting the water or digging holes in the river bed to keep more of the stuff than they need.'

Crocker turned suddenly to look at his companion.

'Wonder if it was Shallow Creek hands who

jumped Christian Barrett?' he said thought-fully.

Ed Blayney met his stare.

'There's no way of knowing,' he replied smoothly. 'But most likely it was a couple of drifters.'

'Yip,' Crocker agreed. 'I ain't never known anyone makes enemies as easily as Christian Barrett. Even the smallholders don't like him.'

'Who are they?'

'There's a few of them on CM range,' the cook explained. 'There's plenty of room for them and they never bothered Marcus or old man Barrett; but I don't reckon Christian will rest till he's moved them on elsewhere...'

One particularly scorching afternoon they pulled up at the edge of a river that ranged through a copse of cottonwoods.

'There's plenty of greenery round here,' Crocker announced. 'I'm gonna get down and see if I can find any plants for the ranch cooking-pot. Meantime, you get a bucket and fetch some water for the horses.'

Blayney was already aware of Crocker's passion for herbs that he used for cooking and medicinal purposes. He waited for the cook to get out of sight among the cotton-woods before making his way down the steep bank to the water's edge. Once there, he stripped off his shirt and knelt down, then splashed the water over the upper part of his body.

Its coolness took the fire out of his tortured skin for a few blessed moments.

'Blayney!'

He spun round and saw Crocker standing by the side of the waggon. Something had brought the cook back unexpectedly. Blayney struggled to put the shirt back on, but Crocker had already noticed the ugly marks on his body.

'Them's gunshot wounds,' he said gravely. 'Whether you try to hide them or not, they're still gunshot wounds.'

Blayney stood there without saying a word.

'You still got lead in you?' Crocker asked.

Blayney shook his head.

'The doc in Wichita said they were clean when he'd finished, but they'd take time to heal.'

'Let me take a closer look,' Crocker suggested.

'They're okay, just raw that's all,'

'I can see they're raw,' Crocker snorted. 'Only there's raw and raw.'

He went down on one knee at the cowboy's side and ran his hand over the wounds.

'At least three slugs,' he stated knowledgeably. 'But I reckon the doc's right. You'd be green by now if there was lead in you.'

He straightened up again.

'I got herbs back at the ranch that can fix worse than that,' he said.

'I don't want the others to know,' Blayney said in a deadpan voice. 'I didn't want anybody to know.'

It all made sense to Crocker now: the cowboy's pallor and lack of stamina; the young feller must have been at death's door a few weeks before.

'It's okay,' Crocker assured him. 'I don't want to know any more myself.'

SEVEN

What Marcus Barrett liked most about homecoming was the sight of his sister Katy waiting at the open door of the ranch house when he and his brother arrived.

As a show of respect Katy, at eighteen the youngest of the three of them, always greeted her elder brother Christian first, but her warmest embrace was reserved for her favourite, Marcus. Christian Barrett noted this without comment, but noted it none-theless.

Katy was a quiet, intense young girl who devoured the contents of the few books the ranch possessed. She also had a practical side to her nature, and her cooking was one of the features that encouraged cowboys to sign on for work at the CM spread. This time Marcus had managed to barter for a few paperback copies back at Milton; they weren't even brand new, but Katy was as delighted with them as if she'd been given a leather-bound copy of one of the great classics.

Within a few days most of the ranch hands had made their way back onto CM land, and resumed their duties of patrolling, seeking out sick or injured animals and rounding up mavericks that had strayed off the beaten track.

Marcus Barrett was also riding the range when a cowhand brought him word that Jensen, Pope and Young had returned to the ranch house. Marcus was both puzzled and displeased by the news.

'Don't say Christian didn't pay them what was owed them at Milton,' he wondered.

He rode immediately back to the house,

but saw no sign of the gunslingers. Instead of greeting him with the usual smile, his sister Katy was tight-lipped and tense when he arrived.

Marcus didn't need to inquire what was eating her. Katy had taken an instant dislike to Jensen when Christian had hired him prior to the cattle drive. To complicate matters, Jensen seemed impervious to her coldness and made a point of hanging around the girl whenever he had the chance.

Marcus went straight into the small room where the ranch ledgers and accounts were kept. This was Christian Barrett's favourite spot and special preserve, since he preferred to avoid the heavy outdoor work on the range.

Christian was standing at a window, looking through a heavy ledger. He didn't bother to look up as his brother came in.

'I hear that Jensen and the others were here earlier,' Marcus said.

Christian was still intent on his reading.

'They still are,' he informed his brother.

'They're over at the bunkhouse.'

Marcus could feel his temper rising.

'What the hell's going on, Christian?' he demanded. 'Those fellers were taken on as extra guns on the trail.'

His brother looked up from the book and gave him a cool stare.

'We still need extra guns, Marcus,' he replied.

'In hell's name, why? We ain't never needed them before.'

Christian Barrett threw the ledger onto the top of the writing-bureau.

'I did some talking to folk while we were in that railroad town,' he said. 'Folk who know what's going on outside these parts. The plains are filling up with longhorns, Marcus. Soon there ain't going to be enough room for them all. When that happens, the only ranches that'll survive will be the ones that have taken plenty of precautions.'

'There's plenty of land,' Marcus objected.

'So far,' his elder brother corrected him.

'But I'm thinking of the future – yours, mine and ... Katy's.'

He introduced their sister's name with calculated cunning. Personally he didn't give a fig for her future, but he knew the best way to get round Marcus.

'Well, what are you planning on doing?' Marcus asked grudgingly.

'In the first place I want to show the other ranches, and especially the Shallow Creek, that we cain't be squeezed or pushed around. When they see that we've kept Jensen, Young and Pope on the payroll they'll read the signs well enough.'

Marcus shook his head sadly. He knew that much of the trouble between the two ranches was the result of personal animosity between Christian Barrett and Matthew Kemp.

'There ain't no real problem between the Shallow Creek and us, Christian,' he pointed out. 'What happened up at Milton was just high...'

'There ain't going to be no problem,

either,' his brother retorted. 'Not once we've put a fence between us.'

'A fence?'

'That's right,' Christian affirmed. 'It's what's happening elsewhere. It's the only way to stop cattle from straying and it cuts down on the need for hands.'

But we've already taken on three new and unwanted hands, Marcus thought bitterly. However, he acknowledged that his brother was more intelligent than himself; he was just a simple cowman, happy in his work and only planning as far as the next drive. Maybe Christian was right to prepare for the future; he'd obviously given the matter some thought.

A sudden thought crossed the younger brother's mind.

'It's going to cost money to keep three gunslingers on the ranch,' he said. 'And they won't want to do any heavy work.'

Christian turned away and looked out of the window at the declining sun.

'I'll worry about that,' he said curtly.

Marcus didn't like his tone. Although the younger brother, he still did the lion's share of work on the spread. He remembered the look on Katy's face as she'd greeted him just now.

'Christian...'

'Yes?'

'If you have to have those three fellers around, make sure they keep away from the house...'

EIGHT

Unexpectedly the three gunslingers showed little desire to hang around the ranch-house as they'd done prior to the cattle drive. To Marcus Barrett's satisfaction most days they saddled up early and were not seen again until nightfall. The young rancher would have been less pleased if he'd known what the gang were up to.

Christian Barrett, meanwhile, seemed to have grown in stature since the incident at Milton. It was the first physical mauling he'd had in his life, and for a while it kept his spirits low. But now that he knew the price his three assailants had paid for their spree of violence he felt strangely strengthened. He'd finally come to terms with himself; he'd never be physically hard himself but he realized that he had the intelligence and cunning to make up for it, with Jensen, Pope and Young who were never difficult to find when you had the money to pay for their services.

The gunslingers' first mission was to visit the half dozen or so smallholdings scattered around the CM range. Christian Barrett did not accompany them on their visits, but he primed them in advance and rehearsed them carefully in the attitude they were to adopt towards the homesteaders.

The first call was at the Lakins' place, a small but comfortable cabin at the mouth of a watered creek. The Lakins were a couple in their forties, but had no children. Shad Lakin came out to meet the horsemen as they rode up, and his wife stood in the shade of the porch shielding herself from the midday sun.

Shad Lakin had already seen the gun-slingers when he'd visited the Barretts a month or two earlier; he didn't like the look of the men, but they did work for his neighbours, so he immediately offered them the traditional frontier hospitality of food and drink.

Jensen shook his head unsmilingly and turned down the offer.

'We've got work to do,' he explained brusquely, taking a good look round as he spoke.

He noted the chickens roaming freely and numerously about the yard and also the small herd of goats corralled at the side of the cabin.

'Mr Barrett wants to know how much live-stock you got grazing on his land,' Pope informed the smallholder without ceremony.

'Livestock...?'

'That's right, livestock – cattle, poultry, dogs. And don't make the count too low,' Jensen broke in, "cause we'll be back to check that your figures tally.'

Bess Lakin listened in silence, fearful of what the request might mean.

'Why should they want to know that?' her husband demanded. 'Anyways, which Mr Barrett are you talking about – Marcus or Christian?'

Jensen ignored half the question.

'Mr Barrett wants a grazing payment for all your livestock,' he said. 'Five dollars for cattle and horses, and a dollar for smaller animals.'

Shad Lakin turned to look at his wife. His dismay was mirrored in her face.

'But that ... that'd ruin us,' he protested. 'The Barretts got no written claim to this land; everybody knows that.'

Young nudged his horse forward until he towered over the homesteader.

'You got a written claim, mister?' he inquired, resting his hand on the handle of his Colt.

'Nope,' Lakin conceded. 'I got no claim in writing, but...'

'Then keep your mouth shut and start counting,' Young advised him. 'We'll be back in a week for the figures ... and the money.'

The first place the gunslingers encountered any kind of resistance was the Ransom homestead. Old man Ransom was in his fifties, but his son Pete was a lithe young man in his twenties.

Ransom received news of the levy in the same way as the Lakins. He was still pondering over an answer when his son came out from the barn leading a mild-eyed mule on a rope.

Pete Ransom eyed the gunslingers cautiously. They were strangers and their expressions bode no good for him or his father.

'What's going on, Pa?' he asked.

'These three fellers reckon they work for the CM spread,' old man Ransom informed him.

If that's true, Pete Ransom thought, why this air of tension? The three men didn't look like cowhands to him.

'How's Kathy Barrett?' he asked suddenly.

Jensen leered at him.

'If you mean Katy Barrett,' he replied. 'She's fine; still cooking and reading those books of hers when she's got the time.'

The reply proved that the men knew the Barretts well, so why was his father looking so worried?

'We've just been explaining the new deal to your pa,' Pope volunteered. 'You've been having things too easy, living under the protection of the CM ranch without paying a cent for it.'

It took a moment for the gunslinger's words to sink in.

'What's this new deal you're talking about?' Pete inquired.

The three men stayed silent while the

cowboy's father explained the gist of it to him.

'I've explained that we ain't gonna be able to pay,' the old man complained. 'Things is bad enough as it is.'

Pete Ransom could feel his temper rising inside him. It showed in the colour rising to his face. Jensen could read the signs, and didn't want the youngster to go for his gun; Christian had urged them to use restraint for the time being.

'Keep your hands where I can see them, son,' he warned.

At the same time Young drew his gun smoothly and levelled it at old man Ransom's chest. Pete realized the hopelessness of the situation; he and his father were sitting ducks. All he could do was stand there and glower at the three horsemen and dream of vengeance.

Meanwhile, Pope felt he was missing out on the action.

'I can understand you being worried about not being able to pay the levy on all your stock,' he said genially. 'So I reckon we should help you out somewhat.'

He slid his .45 from its holster and drew his horse up alongside the docile mule that was standing patiently alongside its owner. He raised the barrel of the gun and pressed it against the side of the mule's head. The gun exploded with a dull thud and the mule shuddered before falling forward onto its front legs.

Pope sheathed his gun.

'Reckon I just saved you five greenbacks,' he told the homesteaders with a cold grin.

NINE

The cowhands on the CM ranch became aware of a subtle change of atmosphere as the days went by; Christian Barrett was becoming more and more assertive in his direction of the spread.

It wasn't that they saw any more of him; he remained locked away in his office as before, but the orders that reached them through Marcus Barrett bore the distinctive mark of Christian's personality. No longer were they to drive Shallow Creek strays back where they came from, although that was one courtesy the two ranches had always observed despite the enmity between Matthew Kemp and the elder of the Barretts. From now on they were to let the mavericks be, the implication being that by next roundup the Shallow Creek brand would have faded enough for a skilled brander to superimpose the CM mark.

Marcus Barrett's new role was more that of foreman than rancher. However, the younger brother accepted the situation with good grace. Hadn't he always wished that his brother would take more of an interest in running the ranch and leave him free to do what he liked best – riding the range?

Crocker, the camp cook, noted everything but commented little. Back at the ranch his duties were considerably lightened by the presence of Katy Barrett who enjoyed cooking for the few cowpunchers who worked in close enough proximity to come home to base to eat and sleep overnight.

In return Crocker set about the general repairs and improvements that always needed doing to buildings so exposed to Colorado's extremes of climate. Now he had a helper, Ed Blayney, and he was pleased to see the colour return to the younger man's cheeks and the strength to his body and limbs.

One morning Crocker announced that he was taking the waggon into the nearest out-post of civilization, the township of Chalmer's Hill. Apart from supplies for the ranch and ranch-hands, Katy Barrett had given him a fair-sized list of her own requirements.

'It'll take till noon to make the town,' Crocker remarked to Blayney. 'And I won't be back till nightfall. D'you fancy keeping me company?'

'Will Mr Barrett mind us both going?' Blayney inquired.

He could only be referring to Christian Barrett, since Marcus had left the ranch for the range at the crack of dawn. Crocker's spittle rolled along the dusty ground in a ball.

'I ain't even gonna ask him,' he replied.

They rode side by side on the driving board of the waggon, with Crocker holding the reins. The countryside was undulating and interesting and occasionally the cook pointed out an unusual feature or told a story relating to it. Eventually he threw his free arm out in a broad arc.

'We're skirting Shallow Creek land now,' he informed his companion. 'Did you notice a track about a mile back?'

Blayney nodded his head.

'Well, that leads straight to the Kemp ranch-house,' Crocker said. 'Used to go there a lot once, before this crazy business between Christian and Matthew. Had some good times there, too,' he added regretfully.

Blayney had already heard the story so there was no point in pursuing it. Instead, he changed the subject.

'I'm surprised Miss Katy didn't come along herself to shop,' he remarked. 'Most young women would jump at the chance to visit town.'

Crocker gave a short laugh.

'Who'd have fed the men with her and me in town?' he asked.

Blayney shrugged his shoulders.

'I could have driven her in,' he said.

Crocker turned to him and grinned.

'She don't know you, Blayney,' he said pointedly, but without malice. 'None of us know you.'

The cowboy got the message. It was true. Since he'd been at the ranch he'd volunteered no information about himself and nobody had pestered him for any. He felt a curious sense of gratitude that he'd been taken in on trust alone.

They rode on in silence until the sun was almost at its zenith. As they turned a bend in the trail they saw a fork ahead of them. Crocker knew that it led off to the Garieta spread, but he was more interested in the group of men who stood and sat around in the shade of a few cottonwoods, with their horses grazing freely nearby. The fellers were all armed to the teeth.

As the waggon approached a tall man rose nonchalantly to his feet and ran his eyes over every detail of the waggon and its passengers.

'Howdee,' Crocker called out in friendly greeting.

The tall man's face cracked open in an arrogant grin. He ignored the upraised arm and spat venomously in the trail dust. Around him nobody had moved but there was a definite air of hostility in the group.

'Keep your eye on our backs,' Crocker muttered under his breath as the waggon went by.

It was only when they'd opened up a gap of some two hundred yards that Crocker began to breathe more easily. He glanced behind him at the men, who didn't seem to have moved an inch. Then he looked sideways at Blayney who hadn't said a word throughout.

Blayney's face was tense and wet with sweat. Crocker had seen the signs before – the sweat on Ed Blayney's face was the cold sweat of fear...

TEN

The two men drove the rest of the way in silence. Crocker didn't even speak when the township of Chalmer's Hill hove into view. He drew the waggon up in the main street and only then turned to address his companion.

'I got to get my money out of the bank,' he said. 'Then we can go slake our thirst before getting the chores done.'

Blayney merely nodded his head. He was

still standing like a statue by the side of the waggon when Crocker got back from the bank, his shirt pocket bulging with notes.

'Let's grab a drink,' the cook suggested to Blayney, who looked like he could use one.

The saloon was empty apart from the bartender reading a newspaper behind the counter. To Crocker's surprise Blayney only asked for a beer; by this time the cook was feeling a little jittery himself so he downed a whiskey and asked the barman to refill it at once.

'You meet some rough-looking hombres on the trail nowadays,' Crocker observed sombrely.

'Yeah.' Blayney's face was still set and tense, but he sipped his beer quietly and didn't gulp it down. Crocker could see that his companion wasn't in the mood for conversation, so he took a piece of paper from his pocket and began to peruse it. It was the list Katy Barrett had given him and his heart fell as he read it.

'Goddam it,' he grumbled. 'There's a lot

of things here I can only get in one of them women's stores; and they ain't the kind of place I like to be seen in!'

He looked up from the list and caught sight of someone passing outside the saloon window.

'Wait here, Blayney,' he muttered. 'I think I just got lucky.'

Crocker almost flew out of saloon and along the sidewalk until he caught up with a slim young girl of about eighteen years of age.

'Miss Garieta,' he called out, and the girl stopped in her tracks.

'Oh hello, Señor Crocker,' she said with a smile. 'How is Katy Barrett?'

The cook took his hat off as a mark of respect for the beautiful young lady.

'It's Miss Barrett I wanted to see you about,' Crocker told her. 'It's about this godd ... this list she's given me.'

He blurted out his tale of woe and waited for her reaction.

'Of course I'll help,' she laughed, glancing

at the list. 'I have to go into most of these shops for myself.' Suddenly Crocker realized that Rosita Garieta wasn't looking at him. He looked back over his shoulder and saw Ed Blayney standing there.

'Oh, this is my friend Ed,' he told her. 'Ed Blayney. He works on the Barrett ranch. Ed, this is Miss Garieta.'

When the girl held out her hand the cowboy was almost afraid to take it, so delicate did her beauty appear to him. As the girl looked into his eyes she could read a vague disquiet in them that both intrigued and attracted her. Her hand remained in his for a few moments until Crocker coughed diplomatically and brought her back to reality.

'I ... I'll be about an hour,' she stammered. 'Shall we meet back here?'

'Will you need a hand carrying the stuff?' Crocker inquired, ever practical.

'No, Jaime is with me to help,' she replied and Blayney's spirits fell. Who was Jaime ... her feller, her husband?

The girl smiled a farewell and walked

81

away from them. Blayney just stood there watching her as if in a daze.

'Well, there's plenty of other things for us to get apart from Miss Katy's list,' the cook pointed out briskly. 'Let's get going or we'll keep Miss Garieta waiting, and she'll be wanting to get back before dark.'

For the next hour Blayney was kept busy carrying Crocker's purchases to and from the stores waggon. As the latter filled up Blayney had to climb up onto it and pile sacks carefully one on top of the other so that they wouldn't be jolted off on the return journey.

'Hey you, young feller!'

Blayney looked down and saw a short, stocky man standing at the side of the waggon. The man was well past his prime but the silver badge he sported on his shirt declared him to be town marshal of Chalmer's Hill.

'These here's CM horses, ain't they?' he demanded.

'That's right, they are,' Blayney replied.

'How come I don't know you, then?' the marshal asked. His tone of voice was straight but not aggressive.

'I'm new on the ranch,' the cowboy replied.

'I see,' the lawman said. 'Which one would you be – Jensen, Pope, or the other one?'

'He ain't either of them critters, marshal,' a voice said.

The lawman turned and saw Crocker crossing the street towards them. The two men smiled at each other and shook hands cordially.

'Meet Ed Blayney, marshal,' the cook informed him, then shouted up to the cowboy who was still perched on the waggon. 'This is Marshal David Staples, the most ornery lawman west of Kansas City!'

Blayney nodded his head, but remained where he was.

'Blayney ain't no gunslinger, marshal,' Crocker went on. 'He's about as fond of trouble as I am.'

Staples was watching the stranger closely.

He didn't think that Crocker would lie to him, but he was a shrewd judge of character and to his mind there was something about Blayney that made him a man to be wary of. Maybe Crocker knew something that he didn't, or maybe Crocker was wrong in his appraisal.

'He ain't one of Christian Barrett's angel-faces, then?' Staples remarked with a touch of sarcasm.

'Nope, he ain't,' the cook affirmed. 'In fact it was Marcus who offered Blayney the job.'

For a moment it looked as if the lawman was going to discuss the set-up at the CM spread further, but at that point Rosita Garieta emerged from one of the shops carrying a heap of purchases in her arms.

Without a word, Blayney had leapt down from the waggon and was hurrying along to where the young girl was standing. He was beaten to her, however, by a young lad in his early teens whose skin was as dark and olive smooth as hers. As Rosita unloaded the purchases onto the young lad she noticed

Ed Blayney standing there helplessly.

'Jaime,' she said. 'Let Señor Blayney help you with those things.'

She turned and smiled at the cowboy.

'Jaime is my brother,' she said. 'He looks after me.'

The youngster grinned proudly and set off towards a buggy parked halfway towards Crocker's waggon.

'You'd better come, too,' the girl said. 'After all, half the shopping is yours.'

When the goods were duly sorted out Blayney regretfully left the Garietas and carried his share of the goods back to the waggon. As he approached the marshal was already on his way back to the jailhouse, and Blayney realized for the first time that the lawman was lame.

'I was just telling Staples about them fellers we met on the trail,' Crocker informed him. 'The marshal's heard about them; they been causing trouble to travellers, usually lone travellers.'

Blayney loaded Katy Barrett's merchandise onto a free space on the waggon.

'Can't he do anything about them?' he asked.

Crocker shook his head.

'Staples was a stage driver in his younger days,' he explained. 'He had a pretty bad fall and shattered his leg and that put an end to his working days. He cain't even ride a horse properly so there's no way he can go chasing outlaws.'

Blayney was still trying to work out what possible use a man like Staples could be as a town marshal when Crocker called out to Rosita Garieta and her brother:

'The marshal reckons we should ride along with you part of the way. There's some fellers on the trail who may be up to no good.'

The two Garietas accepted the offer gratefully. As they explained, they'd encountered no-one on the way into town, but company was always welcome.

The two vehicles rolled along side by side with Jaime at the reins of the buggy. Crocker meanwhile continued his story about the marshal of Chalmer's Hill, partly from love of talking and partly to disguise the fact that he was feeling somewhat nervous about meeting the group of drifters again.

'Staples was always going to be a strange choice for marshal,' he said, 'even without his disability. For one thing, nobody can ever recall him drawing his gun in anger; he's the sort of man who prefers to talk sense into you rather than shoot you down.'

'What if the other man doesn't want to listen to sense?' Jaime asked suddenly, though Crocker had been talking to Ed Blayney.

Crocker turned to the youngster.

'Chalmer's Hill is one of the most peaceful townships I know,' he said. 'That's a lucky break for Staples, though some folk say that it's the marshal's common sense that makes the town what it is.'

'Have you ever met Mr Wyatt Earp?' Jaime asked, eager to talk to men of the world.

'Nope I haven't, son,' Crocker admitted.

'How about you, Blayney?'

The cowboy merely shook his head. He appeared to be deep in thought and in no mood to join in the conversation. The cook turned his attention back to the Spanish lad.

'From what folk say about Earp,' he commented, 'he's the sort of lawman who causes more trouble than he solves, and there's others like him in the West.'

As he finished speaking he looked again at his companion. He wished he could read Blayney's thoughts. Was the cowboy going to be paralyzed with fear if they had the bad luck to run into those same fellers?

To Crocker's consternation the gang of drifters were in exactly the same place as they'd last seen them. However, this time the man who was obviously their leader moved out into the middle of the trail to confront them as they approached. The drifter had taken off his jacket and the white handles of his six-guns showed up clearly on his hips.

'You'd better take the reins, Ed,' Crocker

muttered tersely.

He glanced at Blayney and saw the tension in his face.

'Pull up,' Blayney told him.

Jaime Garieta heard the command and also reined in the mare pulling the buggy.

Blayney jumped swiftly to the ground and for a moment Crocker thought he was going to run for it. However, Blayney walked slowly in an arc away from the two vehicles. All the while the drifters' leader watched him closely, but without too much concern. In fact, when the man spoke it was to Crocker that he addressed his remarks.

'I see you're well stocked up,' he observed, and Crocker regretted that he hadn't picked up his rifle as soon as he'd seen the drifters in his path.

'If it's food you fellers want,' the cook pointed out, 'any ranch around abouts will give you the usual hospitality.'

The drifter grinned unpleasantly.

'We can take anything we want,' he said.

'But we're more interested in any money you're taking back in wages for the cow-pokes.'

Crocker just sat there tight-lipped. He had in fact drawn money out of the bank on Marcus Barrett's instructions.

'Well, if you ain't talking,' the drifter went on, 'maybe the pretty young lady will... Jethro, get her off the buggy.'

An older member of the gang moved rather hesitantly towards the Garietas. None of the others moved and it was obvious that their whole strength lay in the personality of their leader.

'Don't touch her, Jethro...'

It was the first time Ed Blayney had spoken and his voice sounded hoarse. Crocker glanced across him and saw the beads of sweat standing out on his forehead. The man issuing orders could see them too and his lips curled contemptuously.

'Do like I say, Jethro. D'you want me to get mad at you?'

Jethro still stood there not daring to move,

and the rest of the drifters merely looked on.

'Just stay right there, Jethro,' Blayney advised him. 'That way you can't get hurt.'

The gang leader's eyes narrowed as he felt his authority threatened.

'You're in my way, cowboy,' he spat at Blayney.

The colour had drained from Blayney's face but he met the drifter's gaze square on.

'It's your play,' he said quietly. 'You going to make it?'

The two of them were standing like statues as the spectators watched with bated breath. As Crocker told it afterwards, the movement and the explosion were all one. The drifter's gun dangled uselessly in his hand as he staggered backwards with a .45 slug in his chest. Even before he fell Blayney's Colt was already covering the members of his gang.

'Jethro,' he said.

The man licked his parched lips.

'Yeah?' he croaked.

'You're a wise man,' Blayney told him. 'Now bury your friend here, and then get the hell away from these parts.'

ELEVEN

If Crocker was impressed by Ed Blayney's showing in the gunfight he was just as impressed by the cowboy's behaviour over the next few days. Many a man would have taken to boasting about his exploit and even exaggerating his prowess. Blayney, on the other hand, kept silent about the whole affair and Crocker, respecting his friend's reticence, similarly avoided mentioning the incident to the other cowpunchers or even to Katy and Marcus Barrett.

Crocker did notice one change in Blayney since the journey to Chalmer's Hill. It was as if a weight had been removed from the cowboy's mind. Blayney was suddenly less withdrawn and more communicative and generally more relaxed.

Crocker prided himself as a student of his fellow man, and he guessed that the violent confrontation on the trail had removed some hidden fear lurking in the cowboy's mind, some lack of confidence, maybe even a suspicion of cowardice. Crocker thought back to the wounds he'd tended on Blayney's body; they'd been bad enough, but sometimes mental scars took even longer to heal than physical ones. He'd known some to take a lifetime.

In Blayney's case a sudden crisis had brought his problems to a head; if he'd let them overwhelm him the result would have been disastrous. Crocker shuddered to think what would have happened to them, and to the girl, if Blayney had failed the test.

At the back of Crocker's mind lurked the suspicion that it was Rosita Garieta's presence that may have tilted the balance in Blayney's favour. Men heavily outnumbered womenfolk on the frontier and often displayed a chivalrous attitude towards the fair sex that they did not always accord their fellow men. That afternoon Rosita Garieta had been in danger, either from a bullet or from the unwelcome attentions of the gang of drifters. Failure to defend a women was the depth of depravity in many folks' eyes. Crocker himself might well have let the men get away with supplies and money but he knew he'd have picked up a gun to defend Rosita, however clumsily and fatally. Luckily Ed Blayney had been there to take the initiative, so that only one life was lost rather than several.

Less than a week later Marcus Barrett received an invitation from the Garietas for him and his hands to attend a barbecue at the Spaniards' ranch the following Saturday evening. The CM cowpokes received the news with jubilation. Despite Señor Garieta's stern appearance and correctness of manners he was known far and wide as a generous host who treated all his guests with the same hospitality whether they were landowners or saddle-bums. Garieta prided himself also on the stock of the wine and spirits he kept in a cellar underneath one of his barns and when he gave a party the liquor flowed freely and lent an added zest to the eating and dancing that went on long into the night.

Dances and barbecues were welcome distractions from the monotony of cowpunching and riding the range. For many cowhands it was one of the few chances they had of meeting a member of the opposite sex on social terms and maybe holding hands with one of them in a barn dance. Even then the men were likely to outnumber the females five or six to one but it was better than nothing and the merest smile from a pretty girl to a tipsy cowboy would be enough to fill his memories for the next three months.

What most of the CM cowhands dreaded was to be fated to be left behind to watch the ranch in case of mishap. Fortunately for them Christian Barrett decided to turn down the barbecue and stay behind with the three hired guns, Jensen, Pope and Young. For once the gunslingers almost achieved popularity among the ranch hands who were thus freed to enjoy themselves and forget their usual chores in a night of merry-making.

If Marcus Barrett suspected his brother's motives in keeping away from the barbecue he showed no sign of it as he drove the buggy out of the ranch with his sister Katy at his side and a jumble of whooping cowboys riding behind as a ragged escort.

The route they took was a new one to Ed Blayney. Marcus Barrett headed straight down to the river instead of skirting Shallow Creek land and following the trail to Chalmer's Hill as Crocker and Blayney had done a week earlier. The cook explained to Blayney as they rode that the river made a vast loop in Shallow Creek territory, but it was fordable in two places and a trail allowed direct access to Garieta land via a series of creeks and ravines.

In fact by this route the journey took a mere two hours and that without hurrying, which was for the best since the trail was rocky and steep in parts, with plenty of loose gravel underfoot.

They reached the Garieta ranch-house as the Spanish family and cowhands were making the final preparations for the evening festivities. There was no problem about making the return journey in the dark; the eating and drinking would go on through the night until dawn and the guests could make their way home in the safety of daylight with only their sore heads to worry about.

The ranch was already beginning to teem with cowboys, homesteaders and even the occasional town dweller who fancied a night under the Colorado stars. Marcus Barrett and Katy went immediately into the ranch-house to present their compliments to Señor and Señora Garieta but the rest of the CM cowhands kept a respectful distance. Their chance to mingle with the ranch-owning fraternity would come later.

Although nearest neighbours to the Garietas, Matthew Kemp and the Shallow Creek hands did not turn up until dusk. As if by prior arrangement the Barrett and Kemp cowboys did not seek each other out, though in some cases personal friendships crossed the boundaries of inter-ranch rivalry. Soon though, everybody became involved in some way in the running of the barbecue, whether it was feeding the fires or carrying the beef and pork carcasses to where the cooks were waiting. In that way groups got split up and guests began to mingle freely, which was what the party was all about.

The womensfolk had been invited inside the house to tidy up after their journeys and avoid the smoke and dust from the barbecue. When they began to emerge in their colourful frocks and party dresses they became the centre of attention so that a cowboy ceased to notice what feller he was standing next to or sharing a drink with.

By nightfall Ed Blayney had got no more than a glimpse of the lovely Rosita Garieta and he was wondering if she even knew or cared if he was there. Then, as the stars grew so large in the heaven that even the glow of the fires could not obscure them, a hand came to rest lightly on his shoulder and a voice said.

'Señor Blayney?'

He turned and saw a tall, thin man standing at his side. The man's complexion was dark and his clothes black apart from an immaculate white shirt adorned with a slim, black tie.

'I'm Blayney,' the cowboy admitted, wondering what such a distinguished looking gentlemen should want with him.

'I am Antonio Garieta,' the man in black told him. 'I wish to thank you for what you did for my son and daughter the other day.'

He held out his hand and Blayney took it. The Spaniard's grip was boney and strong, despite the fact that he couldn't be far short of sixty years of age.

'I was just along for the ride,' Blayney said awkwardly. 'It was Crocker's idea to ride along with Rosita and er ... Jaime. Do you know Crocker?' he added, anxious to draw attention away from himself. 'He's camp cook on the Barrett ranch.'

'Indeed I do,' Garieta replied. 'Señor Crocker has sometimes treated members of my family with his herbs when one of us has been sick. I have already thanked him for the other day. But is there any way I can thank you with more than mere words, Señor Blayney?'

The cowboy shook his head vehemently.

'There's no need for that, Sir,' he said. 'We were all in the same boat that afternoon. If I could have found another way out I'd have taken it.'

The Spaniard liked the modesty of his reply and decided not to embarrass the cowboy further.

'I shall not forget what you have done, Señor Blayney,' he said quietly. 'And neither will my wife on whose behalf I am also speaking. If you need help some day be sure to let us know.'

In the distance a band had struck up a scratchy fiddle tune. They sounded as if they would need to play a few numbers to get into tune. Still, when the wine and liquor took effect they would either play better or at least sound better to their audience.

Señor Garieta drifted away as unobtrusively as he'd approached. Then Blayney became aware of another presence, a perfumed, exciting presence at his side. It was Rosita Garieta. The girl was wearing a white dress that contrasted wonderfully with her dusky skin, and the red rose on her bosom vied with the redness of her lips.

'Hello, Señor Blayney,' she greeted him. 'I hope you will ask me to dance before the evening is over.'

The cowboy was about to stammer a reply when a group of laughing young girls ran up to Rosita and told her that she was missing out on the fun. Before she could protest they whisked her away in the direction of the music and Ed Blayney felt suddenly alone.

Nevertheless, she had spoken to him and promised him a dance so the future was not altogether bleak. He decided to bide his time and avoid too much contact with his friends from the CM spread who were already making inroads into the free liquor Señor Garieta had so lavishly provided. Fortunately, all the guests seemed equally intent on enjoying themselves and by now Señor and Señora Garieta themselves had taken to the dance floor to demonstrate to any shy young cowhand that the music was a perfect introduction to the lovely young ladies standing around just longing to be asked.

As the night wore on Blayney realized that dancing with Rosita Garieta was not going to be all that straightforward. A new partner presented himself speedily at the start of each number and since excuse-me's were banned in case of trouble between rival males there was no chance for him to cut in during the dance. To add to his problems, the music always seemed to stop with Rosita at the far end of the crowd from where he stood. If Blayney had been an accomplished dancer he could have chosen another partner and manoeuvred her around in pursuit of his prize, but the cowboy had spent his life learning other skills that were only called for in confrontations.

Katy Barrett, on the other hand, had only one partner in every dance. He was a slim, swarthy, good-looking youth in his early twenties. This man moved around the floor with a natural style and arrogance that made the rest of the cowboys look like hamstrung bison. Blayney envied him his poise and confidence; if ever he felt himself lacking something, it was now.

Fortunately the tempo of the music changed to barn-dance and it was the turn of the drunker elements of the menfolk to charge forward and line up with the rest. In this dance the women were outnumbered by the men who, undaunted, lined up opposite one another if there was no lady available.

Desperate as he was to get on the dance

floor Blayney was lucky enough to see a man in front of him lean over too far to one side and land up outstretched and giggling in the dust. A small timid-looking woman was standing opposite the now empty space and Blayney hastened to occupy it before the same idea entered any of the fuddled minds around him.

'I guess I don't really dance,' he confessed as the lead fiddler began to explain the intricacies of the coming number to the assembly.

His modesty and obvious sobriety appealed to the middle-aged lady, who was still rather shocked by the sudden demise of her previous partner.

'Just follow me,' she said with a sweet smile. 'I'll exaggerate the movements a little so that you won't get lost.'

She was as good as her word and proved to be an excellent teacher. By the time he'd moved on to his next partner Blayney had attained a level of proficiency he'd never have expected. From partner to partner he improved in stages until finally he realized his goal and caught up with the beautiful Rosita Garieta.

Rosita was a good dancer, too, but at least by now he could keep up with her and her smile told him she was glad he was there. The end of each section of the barn-dance was a procession of the dancers under the arched and upstretched arms of two partners who then went scurrying back to the front of the column. When he and Rosita passed under the arch, however, she held firmly onto his hand and led him quickly off the dance-floor and into the darkness of the night.

They must have run about a hundred yards before they came to a large barn and the Spanish girl paused for breath.

'They won't miss us,' she told him. 'There are so many people there.'

Personally Ed Blayney didn't care whether they were missed or not, but he did hope nobody would come looking for them. It was nice to be there alone with the girl, with the glow of the fires and the distant sounds of the festivities as a back-drop to their solitude.

'Have you ever been in a wine cellar, a real wine cellar?' the girl asked suddenly.

'Nope, I guess I...'

'Come on then!'

He followed her inside the barn door which was half-open. She fumbled a moment in the darkness then.

'Take hold of this lamp.' she told him. 'And don't drop it; it's got a glass cover.'

Some more fumbling and she'd managed to find a box of matches alongside the lamp and had lit one. Blayney pushed the glass to one side and the girl lit the lamp in one go. As its glow strengthened she led him further inside the barn until she came to a wooden door lying flat out on the earth.

'That's the entrance to the cellar,' she informed him. 'Move it to one side and you'll see the steps.'

Once they were at the bottom of the shallow staircase she paused for a moment.

'We'd better replace the door,' she said.

'Papa does not wish for too many people to know about it.'

Ed Blayney dutifully pulled the door closed over their heads. The cellar was full of large wooden barrels and casks, some of which were lettered in Spanish.

'Did your father make all this stuff?' Blayney asked in amazement.

'Oh no,' the girl laughed. 'Some he produces here but most he brings in from outside.' She tapped one of the barrels and it sounded empty. 'Anyway, not all of them hold liquid.' she confessed. 'Sometimes my father just keeps a barrel because it comes from Spain and it reminds him of his youth before any of us children were born.'

She went up to a table which held several small tin cups.

'These are for tasting,' she informed her companion. She went over to one of the smaller casks and turned a small tap at its base. 'This is sherry,' she said, handing him the cup. 'It is very good.'

She waited for him to drink, but he just

stood there looking at her. At last she seemed to realize what was wrong. She moved closer to him and let him put his free hand on her shoulder.

'You will spill your drink,' she warned, but tilted her face up to his and let him kiss her on the lips. He kissed her again, more warmly and lingeringly. To hell with the drink, he thought...

When they eventually left the cellar Blayney felt almost drunk from the girl's perfume and warmth of her body. He closed the trap door regretfully while Rosita held the lamp for him.

'*Quien va?*'

The voice startled them. Blayney spun round and saw the knife blade glint in the lamplight. He shoved the girl to one side to shield her with his body.

'Carlos,' Rosita said angrily. 'You frightened us!'

She raised the lamp in the air as she spoke and Blayney could make out the features of the swarthy young man he'd seen dancing so well an hour earlier. He wasn't alone either. Katy Barrett was standing in the half-shadows behind him. She looked as bewildered as Ed Blayney felt.

'What are you doing here, Rosita?' Carlos Garieta demanded, the knife still gleaming in his hand.

'I gave Señor Blayney a glass of Papa's sherry,' his sister replied firmly. 'Anyway, what were you doing in the barn?'

Carlos Garieta looked straight past her and fixed his gaze on Ed Blayney.

'You should be more careful, amigo,' he said coldly. 'I could have put this knife into you before your gun was clear of its holster.'

Blayney met his gaze.

'I know,' he replied. 'I saw a Texan killed like that once in El Paso. But before he died he gunned down the Mexican who'd thrown the knife and another two Mexicans who were unlucky enough to be with him...' The remark struck home and Garieta's eyes blazed with anger.

'I am a Spaniard, señor, not a Mexican,'

he snapped. 'The blood in my veins is *sangre castiza*.'

At that point Katy Barrett wisely moved forward and looped her hand around the Spaniard's arm.

'Carlos,' she reminded him gently. 'Mr Blayney is my friend and Rosita's too.'

The two girls smiled across at each other. Both wanted to defuse the situation. Rosita was only too aware of her brother's hotheadedness, and she'd already seen the drastic way in which Ed Blayney responded to threats.

Fortunately, at that moment a disturbance erupted over in the direction of the dancing: men were shouting and women were screaming as if a fight had broken out.

Carlos Garieta's knife vanished as swiftly as it appeared.

'I must go see if my father needs help,' he told Katy Barrett. 'Wait here with the others.'

As it happened, Señor Antonio Garieta was nowhere near the trouble when it flared up. The same could not be said for the rancher, Marcus Barrett.

A few of the homesteaders on CM land had by now drunk enough to loosen their tongues and quicken their tempers. Most vociferous among them was young Pete Ransom, who'd seen his pet mule shot in the head by the hired gun, Pope.

Ransom cornered Marcus Barrett as the young rancher was tucking into a chicken leg and meaning no harm to anybody. Before Marcus could even reply Ransom was listing aloud his faults and treachery; meanwhile a small crowd gathered round, including other homesteaders who began to do some muttering of their own.

Marcus Barrett by now had also drunk a fair amount, though liquor only blurred his speech and sent him to sleep. He listened in confusion to Ransom's accusations, about which he knew nothing and was even more astonished to find the other homesteaders siding with his accuser.

Crocker's attention was drawn to the

argument by one of his fellow cowhands. The big man's first reaction was to break through the crowd and extricate his boss before the situation got worse. Unfortunately, some of the homesteaders were so riled that they resented his presence and began to jostle him. Crocker was a mild man, but when a punch bounced off the side of his head he responded in kind and flattened the cowboy who'd thrown it. That was the signal for the mayhem to become general.

When Ed Blayney reached the scene, closely followed by the two girls, the Shallow Creek cowpunchers had already thrown their weight behind the homesteaders. The CM hands were fighting on the retreat and some of them were starting to take a beating.

At last the inevitable happened. A CM hand landed hard on the ground a few feet from where Blayney stood. The man's nose was streaming blood but his opponent was still pursuing him.

As he got to his knees the CM cowpoke drew his gun.

'Hold it!'

The barrel of Ed Blayney's Colt came to rest on the side of the man's forehead.

'Drop the gun...'

The man did as he was told and his .45 fell from his fingers. Every head had turned at the sharpness of Blayney's commands. For a moment nobody moved, then Matthew Kemp called out to his men from his vantage point some distance away.

'Back off fellers,' he told them. 'I don't want none of you getting gunned down by Barrett's hired killers!'

TWELVE

A week later two Shallow Creek hands were patrolling a stretch of land that constituted the border between their ranch and CM range. Of course, the border was a notional, invisible one since marker stones were few and far between.

In fact the area was generally regarded as no-man's land by cowpunchers of both ranches. If they chanced to meet there they hailed one another courteously, and if they happened to be old friends they might share a smoke or a yarn about the goings-on in the locality.

The two Shallow Creek men in question were Daltry and Winstone, both of whom had worked for Ma and Matthew Kemp for some time. Daltry was a feller in his forties with plenty of experience behind him.

Winstone was only in his late teens, but he'd joined the ranch at the age of twelve and the Kemp family was the only one he knew; he was consequently devoted to them.

At a point about a mile from the river bend the two cowboys noticed a group of men and waggons in the distance. Daltry had not heard of any travellers in the region so he suggested to Winstone that maybe they'd better get nearer and take a look. They walked the horses forward at a leisurely pace so as not to draw attention to themselves. When Daltry was finally able to see what was going on he shook his head in disbelief.

'Well, I'll be hog-tied!' he exclaimed to his young companion.

Winstone could see as well as Daltry but still couldn't figure out what the men's business was out here in the wilderness.

'Them waggons are filled with wire,' the older man told him. 'Barbed wire that'll hold a stampede. Matthew Kemp ain't gonna like this one bit.'

Winstone viewed the proceedings uncertainly.

'What we better do?' he asked.

Daltry shrugged his shoulders.

'We'd better get back and tell Matthew,' he said. 'Not that he's gonna be able to do much to stop them.'

The young cowpuncher at his side could feel the anger rising in his breast. He reached down and drew his rifle from its scabbard.

'What d'you think you're doing?' Daltry demanded as the youngster raised the rifle to his shoulder.

'Just throwing a scare into them, that's all.' Winstone assured him.

The bullet ricocheted off a metal hinge on the leading waggon and sent the CM hands scurrying for cover. Even Daltry enjoyed seeing them jump like that, but he was sensible enough to realize the danger.

'Let's get out of here,' he said tersely. 'In case somebody recognizes us.'

They turned their horses northwards and began to gallop away. To their relief there was no fire from the CM cowhands. They'd put a clear half mile between them and the waggons when suddenly three riders emerged in front of them.

Daltry hoped to skirt them but the riders began to fan out; it was obvious that they knew what they were doing. Even more ominous was the fact that each of the three men seemed willing to confront the oncoming pair of horsemen single-handed, which indicated plenty of confidence in their own ability.

Winstone had summed up the situation in much the same way, and he realized that it was his duty to extricate the older man from the jam he'd got them into.

'Head for the river,' he yelled. 'I'll cover you.'

Daltry had little choice and even less time to argue. The advancing horsemen were gaining ground and would soon be within range. He wheeled his horse round and felt it accelerate on the downward slope to the river. He couldn't take much comfort from that, however, since the pursuing horses would similarly pick up speed downhill. He heard shots behind him, but didn't look back. Winstone had started all of this, let him finish it.

The horse was flecked with foam by the time it reached the water. Daltry urged it into the current and soon it was swimming out of its depth. The minutes seemed like hours until the animal had a footing on the far bank. Daltry immediately sought the cover of a juniper bush. Only then did he glance back to see how Winstone was faring.

The young cowboy had reached the water's edge a hundred yards or so down-stream. He'd discarded his rifle by now and had drawn his six-gun. It was not an effective weapon over long distances but Winstone fired it once or twice and his pursuers hung back a few hundred yards out of respect.

At last Winstone turned his back on them and ploughed his horse into the river. All firing had stopped now and the cowboy's mount sank deep in the water and began to swim. A calmness had returned to the air and also to the watching Daltry; in a minute or so Winstone would be safely across.

The sharp crack of the rifle didn't register for a moment, then Daltry saw Winstone hunch suddenly in the saddle. The horse's back submerged momentarily under the dead weight of its rider, then Winstone's body toppled over into the water and disappeared from view.

The three riders approached the river bank cautiously as Daltry cringed behind the juniper. They must know he was there. All it needed was for one of them to train a rifle on the tree while the other two crossed the river: one downstream, one up. There was no way he'd be able to get away.

To his surprise, they watched until Winstone's body reappeared like a log some hundred yards downstream, then they turned their horses about and headed back in the direction of the waggons.

It was almost as if they wanted Daltry to take the news back to Matthew Kemp...

THIRTEEN

The atmosphere at the CM ranch had been tense since the night of the Garieta barbecue. Marcus Barrett had returned home with his battered cowhands and confronted his brother with the accusations Pete Ransom and the other homesteaders had levelled at him.

Christian Barrett received the news calmly and unsympathetically. He admitted that the hired guns, Jensen, Pope and Young, had visited the homesteads and demanded money from the occupants, but he pointed out that most spreads would not have tolerated squatters on their land in the first place. Furthermore, he accused Marcus of being over-friendly with the homesteaders, who despised his softness and had bitten the hand that fed them.

Christian was well prepared for the encounter, which he'd foreseen would happen; that was why he'd kept away from the barbecue. So Matthew Kemp had shot his mouth off in support of the homesteaders; well if Kemp was so generous why didn't he offer them a share of Shallow Creek land to squat in?

Marcus just stood there open-mouthed.

'Those folk you keep calling squatters,' he stammered. 'They came here on the same waggon train as Ma and Pa. They were their friends.'

Christian shook his head in disbelief.

'Are you saying they can crowd us off our land just 'cause they knew Ma and Pa?' he countered. 'Didn't Ma and Pa work harder than any of them to build up this spread for you, me and Katy?'

Marcus fell silent. He lacked his brother's eloquence and quickness of thought. The more he argued with Christian, the more confusing he found it all.

For once his sister Katy was of no help to

him, for Katy had other things on her mind. The girl had fallen head over heels in love with the eldest son of the Garietas. Since spending the evening of the barbecue with Carlos, Katy's feet had not touched the ground, and not even the dissension between her two brothers could bring her down from the clouds.

Ed Blayney was glad to get a chance to ride away from the ranch house for an afternoon. Since he and Crocker worked in closest proximity to the Barrett family they were very aware of the tension that hung over the ranch like grumbling thunder.

When the cowboy told Crocker that he felt like taking the afternoon off the cook nodded his assent without question. In fact, Crocker felt like taking some time off himself, but he felt responsibility towards Katy Barrett who seemed oblivious to the vibrations around her.

'You go, Ed,' he told Blayney. 'I'll square it with Mr Barrett if he asks.'

There didn't seem much likelihood of

that; for days both Barrett brothers had lived within themselves, hardly addressing a word to Crocker and Blayney. For his part, Christian had always ignored Blayney's presence as if he hated to admit his debt to him; but for the normally cheerful Marcus Barrett to pass the two cowhands without acknowledging them just illustrated how low his spirits had sunk.

However, Blayney put all that to the back of his mind as he trotted his mare to the ford that they'd used when visiting the Garieta ranch the previous week. As soon as the horse was across the river he felt a weight lift from his shoulders. Blayney was highly sensitive to trouble since he usually managed to get drawn into it by his talents with a six-gun. It was good to leave the tension behind, if only for a few hours.

He came across the palomino grazing in one of the creeks leading to the next river ford. He felt his pulse quicken as he dismounted and let his horse wander free. He looked upwards and saw the small log hut perched on a ledge of rock some fifty yards above his head. Fortunately there was a clear trail that wound its way through the shale slopes of the creek.

He was puffing a little when he reached the entrance of the cabin; his body still hadn't recovered its full strength though he was feeling better every day. He waited for a moment before going through the open door.

'Rosita...?'

She got up from her chair when she heard his voice. The room was surprisingly light, with windows at the side of the cabin as well. She was dressed for riding, in blue denim trousers and a white-check blouse with a white scarf at her throat.

'I thought you'd forgotten,' she reproached him mildly.

Forgotten! Blayney had thought of nothing else all week. She moved towards him and he took her in his arms and kissed her.

Finally she broke away and smiled at him.

'I've been coming here since I was a child,'

she informed him. 'But today it's like the first time.'

He let her lead him over to a wooden bench and sat down beside her.

'Let's thank the feller who built this place,' he said.

Rosita's eyes were bright with past memories.

'Paco came here many years ago,' she said. 'Before Papá, even. Paco came from the Basque country of Spain and he spoke his own language to his animals. He could speak Spanish well, and when we were children Papá used to bring me and Carlos here. Paco would share his black bread and goat's cheese with us, and to us it was a feast!'

'Did Paco have any family?' Blayney asked almost in a whisper so as not to break her reverie.

The girl shook her head.

'Nobody,' she said. 'Sometimes he spoke of his *novia* – his girlfriend – back in Spain. He hoped one day to make enough money to return home to the Basque country and marry her; but all Paco had was goats and a few chickens. When he died Papá took his body back to the ranch and buried him there.'

'At least he's among friends,' Blayney remarked, and the girl squeezed his hand.

'That was a lovely thing to say, Ed,' she told him. 'Paco was like one of our own family though he preferred to live alone out here. Papá offered him work on the ranch but he chose to be independent.'

They lapsed into silence for a few moments as Rosita savoured the past and Blayney savoured the present moment. He felt happy and relaxed in the girl's company.

'I don't know much about you, Ed,' she said suddenly. 'Will you tell me about yourself?'

Blayney stared out through the window at the blue sky as if he could read something there.

'There's not much to tell,' he said quietly. 'I guess I'm not a good man like Paco was.'

She turned her dark eyes towards him.

'You're a very good person, Ed,' she told him. 'You risked your life for us.'

'I mean before that,' he explained. 'Do you think I learned to use a gun like that without hurting people along the way?'

'Then they must have been bad people,' she said stubbornly.

He shrugged his shoulders.

'Bad people, good people ... they're all the same when they point a gun at you.'

She could see the furrows deepen in his forehead as he spoke.

'You must forget all that,' she told him. 'Your life always starts today.'

But he didn't want to forget it; didn't want to conceal anything from the beautiful girl at his side. If anyone made him long for a fresh start in life it was her, but first he must make her understand the sort of man he was.

'My old life ended three months ago,' he went on and she didn't try to stop him. 'I was troubleshooting for a rancher in east Kansas. I went into town on business for him and ran into two gunfighters working for a rival spread. They were itching for trouble and I guess that maybe I was as well. Anyways, I ended up with three slugs in my body; I was shot up pretty bad.'

'What about the other ... gunfighters?' Rosita asked.

'I killed them. I had no choice, and they had no choice either; that was the sort of life we led.' Blayney's face was expressionless now but there was a bitter note in his voice. 'My boss didn't even come looking for me when he heard I was hurt,' he said. 'The town council knew the two men I'd killed were hired guns. I was a stranger to them so they took me to be an innocent victim and I never told them any different. They paid the local doc to patch me up and he did a good job. Then I met Crocker in Milton and he nursed me back to health.'

He looked much happier to have got the story off his chest and Rosita felt even closer to him now that she knew the worst.

'In our old religion,' she told him, 'people

used to go to the parish priest and confess their sins and have them forgiven; then they felt much better. You will feel better now that you have told me about your past.'

'I'm more concerned about how you feel, Rosita,' he replied.

She laid her head on shoulder and let him kiss her again.

'I feel good,' she assured him. 'Very good...'

FOURTEEN

Ma Kemp rocked to and fro silently in her cane chair as Daltry recounted the story of the killing down the river. Ma Kemp was a small, shrivelled woman who packed about as much meat as a winter sparrow. However, her eyes were bright and shrewd and what she lacked in physical stature was more than made up for by mental resilience. She'd forged a ranch single-handed out of the harsh plains after her husband died prematurely.

Now her son Matthew was old enough and willing enough to assume the role of ranch boss, but still his mother's personality straddled the Shallow Creek spread like an unseen and protective cloak.

Matthew Kemp was on the balcony with them, listening to the cowpuncher's story with mixed feelings of sorrow and anger. For the moment he kept those feelings to himself since it was to Ma Kemp that Daltry had come to report.

'I didn't get close enough to the varmints to see who they was,' Daltry said apologetically. 'My first thought was to get Winstone away from there after he'd fired the shot.'

Ma Kemp's face betrayed no emotion, though she'd treated Winstone almost as a second son for the past six years. Ma Kemp's principle was rigid: the ranch before any other consideration.

'So they managed to shoot him down from a distance,' the old woman mused aloud.

'Do you think it was a lucky shot?'

Daltry fingered the rim of his stetson nervously.

'It's hard to say Ma'am,' he replied. 'There'd been shooting all along, but of course, we was moving then. I guess that when Winstone reached the river he was a better target.'

'But it still took a good shot,' Ma Kemp insisted.

Daltry nodded his head.

'Yip,' he admitted. 'It was a single shot and a good one. They knew what they were doing all right.'

The old woman's eyes squinted in the dying sunlight as she turned and looked up at her son.

'Rumour has it that Christian Barrett's taken on hired guns,' she said. 'D'you reckon that could be true?'

'I reckon, Ma,' Matthew replied. 'Out at the Garieta barbecue one of Barrett's men drew a gun right next to me and I hardly saw his hand move!'

'The feller who drew the gun is a friend of Crocker's,' Daltry interposed. 'He's the one who stood up to the drifters who tried to hold up Rosita and Jaime Garieta. Crocker's a good man. I don't reckon...'

'If Crocker's so good, why's he working for the Barretts?' Matthew Kemp said sharply.

'There's good and bad everywhere, Matt,' his mother reminded him, but she couldn't help wondering whether the Garietas' saviour was also Winstone's executioner.

She lapsed into silence for a few moments as she made up her mind what to do.

'Get the buggy ready for the morning, Matt,' she said at last. 'You and me are going to call on Marshal Staples.'

Matthew Kemp and his mother reached Chalmer's Hill the next day just in time to hear the solitary church bell summon the townsfolk to morning service.

'Pull up as close as you can to the front of the church, Matt,' she told him.

When he'd brought the buggy to a halt the

old woman jumped down nimbly and brushed the trail dust from her black cloak.

'I'm going inside for a while,' she informed him. 'You can wait for me here.'

He watched her disappear through the door without a shred of curiosity. Matthew Kemp had never been inside a church in his life, nor did he have any inclination to do so. He much preferred to stay out in the street and see the townsfolk pass by and maybe exchange a word with acquaintances.

His mother was equally a stranger to the religious life, or at least had been since her marriage to her actively atheistic husband. Indeed, several of the congregation looked up in surprise as she passed them on her way to an empty pew. Ma Kemp just ignored them, and similarly refrained from joining in the hymn singing and even from listening to the message of the preacher during the sermon.

Instead she let a series of images run through her mind – pictures of a young lad coming to seek work at the ranch some six years before; of him settling into a world of men and developing into a fine young cowboy.

When she left the church with the rest of the congregation she felt strangely better, though she hadn't said a prayer or shed a tear. She brusquely woke her son Matthew from his reverie by ordering him to convey her to the town marshal's office.

Staples struggled to his feet to greet his visitors. Ma Kemp was a prominent local citizen even if she rarely graced the township with her presence. When he'd made sure his guests were comfortably seated he hobbled back to his own leather armchair behind the oak desk that was piled up with paperwork.

'What can I do for you, Ma'am?' he inquired, reaching for his tobacco pouch.

Ma Kemp recounted the story of Winstone's death factually and undramatically. Staples listened sympathetically, but at the end of her story he shook his head sadly.

'You're talking about something that's

outside my jurisdiction,' he told her. 'It'd take the county sheriff to sort the thing out; and we don't see him around these parts once in a mild summer. Besides, there's two sides to the story you just told me. Your man Daltry admits that Winstone fired the first shot.'

'It was a warning shot,' Matthew Kemp broke in angrily. 'They were fencing off the range.'

'It was a shot for all that,' Staples reminded him. 'With the odds stacked against them like that, Daltry was lucky to live to tell the tale.'

Ma Kemp's eyes were perusing the lawman's face and making him feel uncomfortable.

'You won't act, then?' she challenged him.

Staples spread his hands wide on the table.

'I cain't act,' he said. 'No jurisdiction for a start, no clear case either. The Barretts will come up with a dozen witnesses to prove it was self-defence.'

Matthew Kemp's fists were clenched at his side, but his mother was unruffled.

'You could arrange a parley,' she said.

'A parley?' Staples stared at her.

'That's right. You can choose neutral ground and get the parties concerned to attend. I can tell you right now that we'll be there.'

Staples scratched his chin thoughtfully.

'What if the other parties turn it down?' he asked.

Ma Kemp's mouth twisted into a wry smile.

'Then there'll be range war, Marshal Staples,' she told him.

FIFTEEN

It took the lawman almost two weeks of effort to arrange a mutually convenient meeting between the hostile parties from the CM and Shallow Creek outfits. In the meantime the CM cow-punchers continued their fencing work, observed from a respectful distance by Shallow Creek outriders who were still simmering over the death of the young cowboy, Winstone.

The gunslingers Jensen, Pope and Young wisely kept away from the front line for the time being; instead, they spent their time harrying the homesteaders on CM land, exacting the first instalment of the payment that Christian Barrett expected the settlers to hand over at regular intervals for their tenancies.

Crocker and Ed Blayney did their work

around the ranch buildings as usual, though Blayney's absences became more frequent. As Marcus and Christian Barrett seemed to have their minds on more important matters, Blayney's excursions went unnoticed and soon he was meeting Rosita Garieta every other day in their hideout across the river.

Rosita had fallen so deeply in love that she came close on several occasions to blurting out her secret to her family. However, the Garietas were distracted by other things for the time being. Señor Antonio Garieta had taken an active interest in Marshal Staples' attempts to keep peace on the range and he readily agreed to act as host to the planned parley between his two powerful neighbours. In addition, Carlos had put his courtship of Katy Barrett on a formal basis by calling on her regularly and accompanying her on shopping trips to Chalmer's Hill.

Carlos was the eldest of the three Garieta children and Rosita hesitated to declare her own liaison while that of Carlos and Katy

Barrett was still in its infancy. There was also another problem that Rosita chose to push to the back of her mind.

She knew her father was indebted to Ed Blayney for the way the cowboy had defended her and her brother Jaime on their way back from town. However, Antonio Garieta was proud of his ancestry and the *sangre castiza* that ran through his veins. The old man was delighted with the burgeoning romance between his son and a member of one of the most wealthy ranching families in the locality. But what would his reaction be to the news that his daughter was in love with a humble ranch hand, an employee of the family his son might one day marry into?

She thought of discussing her anxieties with her mother, but decided against it. Señora Garieta was kindness itself, but at the end of the day it would be the male head of family who would give his *sí* or no. Consequently Rosita continued to live for the present and to enjoy the precious hours spent with Blayney at the cabin Paco the goatherd had bequeathed them.

Christian Barrett had also done a lot of thinking in the past week or so. Much of the message-carrying between the interested parties had been done by Carlos Garieta, who was glad of the opportunity to visit the Barrett ranch as often as possible. Christian showed no open interest in his younger sister's courtship, but he noted everything in his mind and considered how it would affect the future – not only Katy's future but also Marcus's and his own.

A link with the Garieta spread would be useful to Christian in his ambition to become a power in this corner of Colorado. Then he thought of Matthew Kemp and wondered if Kemp had also foreseen the advantages of closer ties with the Spaniards.

On the appointed day Christian and Marcus Barrett set out for the parley accompanied only by three other riders. What they lacked in numbers they more than made up for in fire power since the three escorts were

Jensen, Pope and Young. From the start, then, Marcus Barrett was placed at a disadvantage; the gunslingers were loyal to Christian and they would back up whatever stance Christian chose to adopt at the meeting.

When they reached the Garieta ranch-house they found Ma and Matthew Kemp already installed in the Spaniards' living room. Marshal Staples was there as well. The half-dozen or so cowboys who'd accompanied the Kemps had been consigned to the ranch chuck-house for a meal. Jensen and his two companions, however, refused such hospitality and chose to remain outside the ranch-house but within easy reach if they were needed.

'The rest of us will only eat when this thing is settled,' lawman Staples declared with a note of irritation in his voice. He was weary after the journey and his gammy leg hurt like hell. At the moment he felt little sympathy for either side.

No objection was raised when Staples

requested Señor Garieta to remain in the room throughout the debate. Staples had only ever worked on stage-coaches and he knew little about ranching. If he had to act as some kind of judge over the proceedings he needed somebody neutral he could turn to for advice.

In fact the portents looked ominous to the town marshal. The easy-going Marcus Barrett was bound to play second fiddle to his elder brother, and Christian had hardly brought his three hired guns with him as ornaments. It looked as if the head of the CM spread was going to lay the law down pretty heavily to Ma Kemp and her son Matthew.

But nothing could have been further from the truth. From the start Christian Barrett asked the Kemps to explain their grievances and when these came out in a flood he listened politely. Then, to everyone's amazement he apologized for failing to see that his previous actions had caused alarm to his neighbours and promised to cease the fence-building immediately.

Next, Christian turned his attention to the matter of the killing of the cowboy Winstone. There was no way, he said, that he could find out which of his men had fired the shot. However, as a gesture of goodwill he promised to dismiss the two members of his outfit who'd drawn their guns at the Garieta barbecue. Marcus Barrett gasped at the decision. Ed Blayney had drawn his gun to prevent bloodshed. Unfortunately, the Kemps were obviously delighted by Christian's show of good faith and Marcus was afraid he'd spoil the goodwill of the meeting if he quibbled over this. For his part, Señor Antonio Garieta realized that Blayney was being treated unfairly, but the Spaniard had agreed to stay as an observer, not to question the decisions reached.

Thus the participants of the meeting sat down to an earlier than expected meal with the Garieta family. It was a happy relaxed occasion; so relaxed in fact that Carlos Garieta suddenly rose to his feet and formally announced his wish to ask Katy Barrett for her hand in wedlock if her two brothers did not object.

Christian Barrett looked across at his younger brother. Marcus merely grinned and nodded his head. Christian then ran his gaze around the whole assembly, lingering a little longer on the lovely face of Rosita Garieta.

'As head of family, I certainly give my consent,' he said with a faint smile. 'But only on condition that Carlos's sister Rosita will consent to be my bride as well...'

SIXTEEN

Ed Blayney received both items of news at the same time. It was Crocker who broke the story to him. Marcus Barrett didn't have the heart to face the cowboy. Instead he summoned the ranch cook and asked him to pay Blayney the wages he was owed.

Crocker learned about the engagement of Christian Barrett to Rosita Garieta from Katy Barrett, who was bubbling with excitement at the prospect of a double family wedding.

Blayney took the twin blows stoically. His presence on the CM ranch had always been a thorn in Christian Barrett's side, since it was a constant reminder of his humiliation at the Milton whorehouse. It was the news about Rosita that really hurt. She could not be in love with Christian Barrett. He could only presume that she was ignoring the feelings of her heart and opting for a secure future. In a way he could understand that and he tried hard not to feel bitter.

Before leaving the bunkhouse he wrote a brief note on a piece of paper, folded it and stuffed it into his shirt pocket. He didn't know how he was going to get it to Rosita; in fact he didn't even know how he was going to get off the ranch himself.

Outside in the yard Crocker was standing

beside the mare Blayney had ridden since he'd come to work for the CM outfit. The mare was saddled up.

'She's yours,' he told the astonished cowboy. 'It's a leaving present from Marcus.'

The cowboy's predicament made him swallow his pride. The mare would at least solve some of his problems.

'Thank Mr Barrett for me,' he said. 'Marcus, that is.'

Crocker nodded his head.

'Where you heading for?' he inquired.

'Well, first I've got an errand to do,' Blayney told him. 'Then maybe I'll head for Chalmer's Hill and look for work.'

He got up onto the horse and Crocker stretched up and shook his hand warmly.

'If you do go to Chalmer's Hill,' the cook said, 'make sure to call on Marshal Staples. Tell him Crocker sent you.'

Blayney wheeled his horse around and urged it forward. He made straight for the river and didn't look back once at the Barrett ranch-house. Within a half-hour he'd reached the ford and crossed the river, heading for the log cabin in the hills. Today he knew Rosita Garieta would not be there, but still she filled his thoughts as he rode along.

It was the first time he'd been alone in the cabin, since Rosita had previously always got there in time to greet him. Instead of being filled with the young girl's beauty and vitality the building was depressingly empty. He'd never noticed how decayed and decrepit it was and somehow it reflected his state of mind.

What did he have to offer a girl like Rosita, he asked himself bitterly. While other men built up a future for themselves he'd relied on his speed of draw to make an easy dollar here and there. Was it any wonder that she'd opted for security and wealth?

He took the note from his pocket and read it for the last time before letting it fall down onto the gnarled surface of Paco's roughly hewn table.

I am headed for town to look for work. Good

luck in your marriage.

That was it. He turned grim-faced and made his way out into the fresh air.

Blayney slept under the stars that night and didn't reach Chalmer's Hill until noon the following day. The small township was bustling with activity since it was market day and stalls were erected the length of the main street.

The cowboy dismounted and led his horse through the crowds. There were some protests from the vendors when the animal brushed against their stands, but Blayney ignored them. He knew what it was like to be without a horse and he wasn't going to lose this one in a hurry.

He reached the jailhouse and was pleased to see the door ajar. Somebody must be in there, or at least in the vicinity.

He tethered his horse to the rail outside the jail and walked up to the door. He looked inside and could see the lawman sitting behind a desk piled up with paperwork.

Nevertheless, the cowboy knocked politely rather than barge straight in.

Staples looked up from his desk.

'Come in,' he said amiably. 'Grab a chair.'

Blayney did as he was told. The marshal eyed him quizzically for a few moments.

'What d'you want?' he asked unceremoniously.

Blayney shrugged his shoulders.

'I don't rightly know,' he admitted. 'I'm looking for work. Crocker from the CM outfit told me to call on you and tell you that he sent me.'

'You the feller who got the boot?'

'That's right. Me and another feller called Leeky.'

'Leeky's a good cowpoke,' the lawman observed. 'He won't be without work for long. How about you?'

'I ain't no cowpuncher,' Blayney said. 'I was just helping Crocker.'

'You're the feller who's handy with a gun, aren't you?' Staples asked bluntly.

Blayney didn't know if it was meant as a

question or an accusation. His colour rose slightly.

'Oh, I've heard all about you,' Staples went on. 'Tell me; can you take orders?'

Blayney met his gaze.

'If they make sense,' he replied and the lawman gave a short laugh.

'Could you take orders from me?' Staples persisted.

'I reckon.'

Staples warmed to his theme.

'Could you patrol the town when my leg's giving me hell?' he asked. 'Could you pick up the rubbish from the street to make the place look tidy? Could you shoot stray dogs that nobody claims? If you can, I'll make you my deputy for thirty five dollars a month and found.'

The cowboy felt his spirits rise as the marshal spoke.

'Where do I live?' he asked quietly.

'I got a place that's been empty since I moved into the jailhouse,' Staples informed him. 'It needs a clean and you may have to shoot a cockroach or two to get law and order, but there's nothing there to frighten a good deputy marshal.'

He reached into a drawer and pulled out a tarnished tin star.

'This is yours,' he said, tossing it across the desk. 'It needs a polish!'

SEVENTEEN

Marcus Barrett was surprised to see his brother saddling up one of the horses in the corral. Christian rarely went out for a ride when he was home, and that made him a liability on cattle drives since he inevitably suffered from saddle sores for the first four or five days.

Marcus leaned on the top rail of the corral and yelled out a jocular greeting.

'Hey, Christian, you going on a roundup all by yourself?'

Christian turned and grinned at him. The two brothers had got on very well since the parley at the Spaniard's ranch. In fact Marcus could not recall such good times since they were small boys running carefree around the ranch buildings, scaring the chickens and turkeys and teasing the mules until the animals would lumber off to seek refuge in one of the barns.

'I'm going to pay a visit to my betrothed,' Christian informed him with a sly wink. 'D'you want to keep me company?'

'Company!' Marcus snorted. 'What company d'you need if you're going to see Rosita?'

Christian tightened the girth and checked to see that the saddle wouldn't slip.

'I'll only spend a few minutes with Rosita,' he assured his younger brother. 'You know how strict her old man is. We'll let him fill us up with that Spanish wine of his and we won't even notice the journey back.'

Marcus liked the idea. It would be a

chance to get Christian away from those stuffy accounts. They'd be able to talk and cement their new-found closeness.

'I'd better tell Katy,' he suggested.

'You do that,' Christian said. 'But if she wants you to take a letter over to Carlos Garieta, tell her no, else she'll be all day writing it!'

At first they rode side by side in silence, just savouring the stillness of the morning air before a breeze could whip up and unsettle the dry trail dust. At last Marcus broke the silence.

'We'll need to build another room onto the house when you marry Rosita,' he said.

His brother shook his head.

'We'll get Katy off our hands the same time, maybe even sooner,' he replied practically. 'That'll give us all the room we need.'

Marcus glanced across at him. Christian didn't seem at all excited about his engagement.

'You're a dark horse, Christian,' he commented.

'You reckon?'

'I reckon. I never even saw you look at Rosita Garieta before the parley.'

When Christian failed to respond to the remark Marcus changed tack somewhat.

'I ain't seen Jensen and the others for a few days,' he observed.

'They're around,' Christian assured him laconically.

The elder brother seemed deep in thought, but Marcus decided that if he didn't speak now he might not get as good a chance again.

'It's a shame about Blayney and Leeky,' he said. 'They were good men.'

'It ain't what we think about them that counts,' Christian pointed out. 'It's what other folks think. Leeky went for his gun out at the Garieta ranch-house. That ain't forgivable.'

'But Blayney stopped him using it,' Marcus objected.

'We know nothing about Blayney,' Christian said. 'Except that he killed a man outside Chalmer's Hill.'

'He was protecting Rosita Garieta,' Marcus protested. 'Crocker told us that.'

Christian was not convinced.

'Then that's good news for the Garietas,' he replied drily. 'But it don't do much for the Kemps. To them Blayney is nothing but a hired killer.'

Like Jensen, Pope and Young, Marcus Barrett thought to himself, but said nothing. Christian obviously was not going to change his mind. At least Blayney had left the ranch with a horse which was more than he'd brought with him.

Over to the right of them he spotted some reels of barbed-wire fencing that had been abandoned by CM cowpunchers a few days before. Christian didn't even seem to notice them.

'We'd better get someone to pick up that wire,' Marcus said. 'In case an animal gets hurt on it.'

His elder brother was staring in the distance.

'You see that outcrop over there?' Christian said suddenly. 'Let's see if I can still race you to it like I could when we were kids.'

Marcus could not help smiling. There was no way his brother could repeat old victories. Marcus more or less lived in the saddle nowadays.

'It's on Shallow Creek land,' he said dubiously.

'So what... It ain't fenced off, is it?' Christian said mischievously as he spurred his horse to the front.

For half a mile or so Marcus humoured his elder brother by holding his own gelding back, but gradually he let the animal lengthen its stride and overtake his adversary with ease. When he reached the foot of the outcrop he pulled up and waited for Christian to arrive.

Christian Barrett was still a hundred yards away when he heard the shot and saw his younger brother tumble from the saddle. He approached the body cautiously and was relieved to see no sign of movement.

Jensen came slithering down the shale slope, rifle in hand. He walked over to the rancher's body and noted with satisfaction the eyes staring unblinking in the strong sunlight.

'He's dead alright,' he informed Christian who'd remained in the saddle. 'You'd better get down.'

Although he'd arranged it all, Christian Barrett still felt as if he was living in a dream. He hardly heard the shot that Jensen put through his horse's heart. He'd have to ride his brother's gelding home. It was all part of the plan.

EIGHTEEN

Three days went by before Rosita Garieta plucked up the courage to ride out to Paco's old cabin in the hills. She'd heard from her father that Ed Blayney was to lose his job with the CM outfit and she wondered what he'd do now.

Her greatest problem, however, was how to explain to Blayney how she'd allowed herself to become engaged to Christian Barrett. It might have helped if she'd fully understood herself how it had happened. Christian Barrett's request had come as a bombshell and she'd been stunned when her father had taken her silence for consent and had welcomed the idea.

Of course, back in Spain in the old days the head of family's word was law, and somehow that tradition still applied in the

Garieta household. Her mother's joy was another problem, since Rosita could not bring herself to disillusion her by revealing her true feelings.

Another consideration was Carlos, who was betrothed to Katy Barrett. If Rosita drew back now, what would be the effect on the other engagement? Christian was head of family at the CM ranch. Would he turn spiteful and obstruct his sister's marriage? Rosita blamed herself for keeping her meetings with Ed Blayney secret in the first place. If her father had been fully informed he would have allowed her to make her own mind up; of that she was confident. Of course, it didn't help her wretched frame of mind to realize that she had in a way contributed to her own misfortune.

Blayney was not at the rendezvous, but his letter was. She read it with a sinking feeling in the pit of her stomach. He was off to town to find work and wished her luck in her marriage!

She sank down heavily into Paco's old

armchair. Was that all Ed could find to say to her ... was that all their relationship meant to him? She read and re-read the note angrily. Well, she would marry Christian then if that was what Blayney wanted.

But a picture of the cowboy kept flashing into her mind and she remembered the look on his face as he'd faced the leering drifter who'd tried to rob them on their way home from Chalmer's Hill. Blayney hadn't wanted to fight, but he'd refused to be cowed by his grinning adversary. It was the same now, she thought, Blayney had been hurt by the news of her engagement and by the loss of his job, but this was his way of facing up to it. What she'd thought of as Blayney's indifference was in fact dignity and stoicism. It made Rosita feel even more sorry for herself and she put her head in her hands and wept.

Crocker rode out with the escort of Pope and Young to retrieve the body of Marcus Barrett. They found him and Christian's dead horse exactly where the elder Barrett had told them.

Pope and Young made a pretence of scouring the outcrop of rock for a concealed sniper, but they both knew that Jensen was miles away by now and heading back to the CM ranch-house by a roundabout route. However, they were convincing enough for Crocker, who accepted Christian's story and distress on face value. He was glad of their company as he loaded the corpse of his boss onto the buggy.

'There's nothing we can do about the horse,' he told the gunslingers. 'It's Marcus we got to see to.'

Pope and Young nodded their heads without interest. Marcus had never done anything for them.

When they got back to the ranch Katy Barrett ran out, white-faced, to meet them. As the buggy came to a halt she pulled the blanket from her brother's body, threw her arms around his shoulders and tried to shake him back to life. All the time she was moaning like a wild animal and Crocker had to come up beside her and draw her gently but firmly away.

Inside the house Christian Barrett was giving his own explanation of what had happened to a couple of CM cowpunchers who'd drifted in hoping for a spot of Katy Barrett's cooking.

'We didn't have a chance,' Barrett told them. 'When I heard the shot and saw Marcus go down, I dismounted and used my horse as a cover. Before the dry-gulcher made off he put a bullet into the horse. Luckily, Marcus's horse was running free and wasn't a good target, else I'd have had to walk home.'

Crocker came into the room, his arms still around Katy's shaking frame.

'Well,' Christian demanded. 'Did you find him like I said?'

'We found him,' Crocker confirmed. 'He's outside. Shall I bring him in?'

The question seemed to bring Katy Barrett to her senses.

'Let me clean his room first,' she said. 'Oh,

my God. It's a mess!'

Crocker was pleased to see her react in this way. Keeping busy was the best antidote against shock.

Christian Barrett's mind was on other things.

'I don't want word of this to get around,' he snapped, eyeing all present grimly. 'This was a revenge killing by the Shallow Creek outfit for the death of that cowpoke last week. I got to give some thought to how we should react.'

They heard the sound of hooves outside in the yard. Christian's right-hand man, Jensen, was riding in dead on time.

Rosita Garieta gave up trying to sleep and rose noiselessly from her bed. It was just like the previous night and the night before that. With all the thoughts swirling around inside her head she wasn't sure that she'd ever sleep again.

The moonlight was streaming in through the window as she dressed hurriedly. It was either this or go crazy she told herself. She stopped only to scribble a note to her parents and explain her madness to them; then she opened the door of her bedroom and walked quietly through the large living room and out into the farmyard.

She decided to lead her horse out of the corral and a few hundred yards down the track before mounting up and riding away. She didn't know what she'd do if someone called her back, but to her relief that didn't happen.

Apart from the moonlight and the maze of stars overhead she was aware of a red glow in the southern sky as she made her way in the direction of Chalmer's Hill. If her thoughts had been less centred on her own immediate predicament she might had pondered over its significance but for the moment she had enough problems of her own on her mind.

'Stewart ... Stewart!'

The Shallow Creek foreman stirred in his bunk. It took him a few moments to realize that someone was calling his name.

'Uh, what's that?' he inquired lazily.

'I can smell burning.'

Stewart's senses sharpened immediately. He breathed in deeply and caught the acid tinge in the air.

'You're right,' he said and threw the bed-clothes from his body.

'Watts, Railton...'

The cowhands didn't need to be summoned; they were tumbling out of their bunks already. One of them ran over to the window and peered out.

'It's the big barn,' he announced. 'It's well alight.'

Stewart began to bawl out orders.

'Tate, you and Watts get down to the well with some buckets. The rest of us'll start beating it out.'

Outside in the darkness Jensen lay flat on his stomach by the corner post of the horse corral. His own horse was tethered to the rail but would pass unnoticed since there were near a dozen of the animals penned on the inside.

Pope and Young had done their work well with only a little brushwood to help them get the fire started. They too had by now drifted into the shadows to admire their handiwork.

Jensen watched without interest the men emerging from the bunkhouse. They weren't his target. He swung his gaze back towards the ranch-house. A light had come on in one of the windows. He raised his rifle from the ground beside him and levelled it at the front door of the house.

The door opened suddenly and a figure appeared carrying an oil lamp. Jensen was too experienced a killer to react too quickly. The person was short and stooped and had white hair. Ma Kemp had come to the door to light the way for her son Matthew.

As Matthew walked by her he turned to say something briefly. For a moment his body was perfectly outlined by the light from the lamp in the old woman's hand.

The rifle cracked in Jensen's hand and

Matthew Kemp staggered to one side. Before his mother could reach him Jensen had fired again and Kemp doubled up with another slug in his guts. The shots were a signal to Pope and Young, and they proceeded to open up on the unarmed Shallow Creek cowhands, who were sitting ducks in the glow of the burning barn.

NINETEEN

Whereas the murder of Marcus Barrett had been kept a close secret, the news of the attack on the Shallow Creek ranch and the death of Matthew Kemp spread across the range like wildfire.

For his part, Christian Barrett viewed the situation with equanimity. Only he and his three hired guns knew all the facts about the killing of Matthew Kemp. If the CM cowhands did suspect anything, they would

167

still be willing to back Christian since they were convinced that Marcus Barrett had been killed by a Shallow Creek bullet. Christian was not particularly concerned about what Ma Kemp might suspect. She had lost not only her son but also some of her best men the other night; the Shallow Creek outfit was no longer a force to be reckoned with.

It was therefore a confident Christian Barrett who turned up at the Kemp ranch-house for the burial of Matthew and the three men who'd died with him on that fateful night. However, Christian took the precaution of surrounding himself by an escort of half a dozen of his own men, including the gunslingers Pope and Young.

The burial took place on a hillside within sight of the ranch-house. A large crowd of plains and townsfolk had made the long journey to pay their last respects to Matthew and extend condolences to the bereaved Ma Kemp, who was pale but dignified in her grief. She walked to the graveside supported on either side by her ranch foreman Stewart and Marshal David Staples of Chalmer's Hill.

Christian Barrett kept himself and his men at a distance throughout the proceedings, but he did instruct one or two of his cow-punchers to spread the word that Marcus Barrett had also been killed recently. That might be enough to convince some folk that rustlers or drifters had caused all the recent mischief on the range.

After the burial Christian meant to slip away quietly but he found himself confronted by a sombre looking Antonio Garieta and his son Carlos.

'May I speak to you, Señor Barrett?' Garieta inquired.

For a moment Barrett thought that the two Spaniards were going to ask him about Marcus' death, but when they led him away from the CM cowhands he realized that they had something else on their minds.

Antonio Garieta did not find it easy to tell his intended son-in-law that Rosita had decamped in the middle of the night and left only a note stating her intention to search for her secret lover.

Christian Barrett received the news with no sense of sorrow but rather as a further problem his agile mind would have to deal with. Señor Garieta and his son Carlos took his silence as a sign of grief.

'My sister has dishonoured the *sangre castiza* of the Garietas,' Carlos declared fervently. 'I intend to avenge the dishonour by killing her lover.'

Christian Barrett turned to him with interest.

'Who is her lover?' he asked.

Antonio Garieta coughed with embarrassment.

'His name is Blayney,' he said. 'He is the man we were grateful to for...'

He couldn't go on. Unlike Carlos, Antonio Garieta still felt gratitude to Ed Blayney, and this escapade of Rosita's filled him more with sorrow than anger. If only Rosita had told him about her feelings for the cowboy.

For Carlos, however, the matter was much more clear-cut; Ed Blayney had betrayed the hospitality of the Garietas and was now jeopardising Carlos' engagement to Katy Barrett.

'I shall kill Blayney,' he insisted stubbornly. 'And I shall bring my sister back to face you and my parents.'

Christian Barrett was no longer in doubt as to the attitude to adopt. Blayney was a threat to his engagement and to his hopes of controlling the Garieta ranch. At the same time Carlos Garieta was within a whisker of marrying into the Barrett family. Well, let him grovel for a while, let him do the dirty work and take revenge on Blayney. When he's no longer useful to me, Christian thought, I can dispose of him as I disposed of my brother Marcus.

'You can't take a killer like Blayney on by yourself,' he said, placing a hand on the young Spaniard's shoulder. 'First I'll find out where he is, then we'll go looking for him together.'

Carlos Garieta smiled his appreciation, but his happiness was short-lived.

'In the meantime,' Christian added. 'I think you should stop calling on Katy until she gets over the death of her brother.'

Jensen was bored. Christian Barrett had decided to leave him at the ranch while the rest went to the Kemp funeral. Jensen couldn't figure out why Christian hadn't taken him along. Superstition maybe, which was one thing Jensen never suffered from.

For the last two hours he'd been alone on the ranch, since Katy Barrett had asked Crocker to join her for a canter on horseback. Jensen didn't often get bored, but he felt a sense of anticlimax after the massacre at the Shallow Creek ranch. If there'd been a town nearby he'd have set off in search of a drink and a woman – and especially a woman. He envied Crocker his closeness to Katy Barrett. If Jensen could have got that close he wouldn't be wasting his time taking her out for a ride. He thought of her lush lips and firm body and felt a sudden anger that they were going to be wasted on Carlos Garieta. Was that what he and Pope and Young were risking their lives for?

He heard a horse gallop into the yard and he jumped from his bunk. Any company would be welcome at the present time. He walked over to the door just as Katy Barrett reined in her sweating horse in front of the house.

Jensen strode quickly towards her.

'Where's Crocker?' he called out, and the girl turned in her saddle at the sound of his voice. Her hair was tumbling loosely over her shoulders and the sunlight made it sparkle like strands of gold.

'He spotted a lame calf,' she replied. 'You know what he's like, he can't see anything suffer.'

As she alighted from the saddle, Jensen stepped forward and put his arm around her waist.

'Thank you,' she said graciously. 'But I can manage.'

She was, on terra firma now, but the gun-slinger didn't release his hold.

'I can manage,' she told him again, but he gave her waist a squeeze before letting go.

'Will ... will you see to my horse?' she asked him to hide her confusion.

She was glad to get away from him and inside the house. Then she heard the door open and Jensen was standing there, a strange smile on his face. She felt suddenly uneasy.

'The hired hands only come in this house when invited,' she informed him, trying to speak with an authority she didn't feel.

He kicked the door shut behind him and leered at her.

'What's wrong...' he asked. 'Don't I put my hand in the right places like that greaseball of yours does?'

Katy could feel her heart pumping and the blood rush to her face.

'Get out,' she ordered him. 'Or Christian will get to know about this.'

Jensen moved towards her, throwing his

hat onto the settee.

'Christian don't like greaseballs any more than I do,' he told her. 'All he's after is the Garieta ranch. Besides, I do plenty of favours for your brother; now I reckon you can do one for me, and I don't care if you do tell Christian when he gets back.'

He made a sudden grab for her and propelled her backwards towards one of the bedrooms. She tried to push him away but he kept coming forward, forcing her to yield ground. Suddenly he lifted her physically off her feet and she felt herself falling on her back onto the bed. Jensen's breath was coming in gasps now, partly from effort and partly from lust.

He held her down with one hand and began tearing at her clothing with the other. The material of her shirt tore where the buttons refused to give way and the sight of her bare flesh was fuel to his frenzied attack.

When she began screaming he only encouraged her.

'Scream, you whore,' he said with relish.

'Scream all you damn well like!'

Then the bedroom door flew open and Jensen felt a hand grab at the scruff of his neck.

'You sonofabitch!'

Crocker hoisted the gunslinger into the air and threw a crippling punch into his solar plexus. Jensen squealed and doubled up like a jack-knife. Crocker hauled him upright again, repeated the medicine and then let him drop to the ground in a heap. He lay there, moaning like a dying beast.

'Are you all right, Miss Katy?'

She pulled her torn garments about her, and fixed her wild eyes on his face.

'He ... he tried to...'

Crocker managed to smile encouragingly at her. 'But he didn't, did he?' he said. 'He didn't have time.'

She began to shake, but pulled herself together at once. Crocker's remark had struck home.

'I hate him,' she said suddenly. 'And I hate Christian, too.'

Crocker at last felt confident enough to put his hand on her arm.

'You can't stay here, Miss Katy,' he told her. 'Not after this.'

She looked up at him helplessly.

'Where can I go?' she asked.

'I'll take you to Marshal Staples,' he said gently. 'Maybe he'll know what to do.'

TWENTY

By the time Christian Barrett and the others got back to the CM ranch-house Jensen had recovered from the worst effects of his beating. When Christian inquired as to the whereabouts of his sister the gunslinger confined himself to saying that she'd ridden off a few hours ago in the company of Crocker.

By nightfall one or two of the cowpokes were beginning to express their concern that

Miss Katy should have been back by now. Christian Barrett dismissed their worries blandly.

'She may have decided to stay overnight in Chalmer's Hill or at a friend's place,' he said. 'Katy knows folk everywhere.'

He spent a restless night, not through grieving over his sister's absence but because his mind was teeming with plans for the future. In fact it would have suited Christian very well if Katy were to disappear off the face of the earth. What if she and Crocker had met up with an accident ... what if someone had exacted vengeance on them for the massacre at the Shallow Creek spread? At least that would put an end to Carlos Garieta's ambitions to marry into the Barrett family.

For his part, Jensen also spent a bad night. He was not worried about Christian finding out what had happened that afternoon, but he was smarting at the way the camp cook had surprised and humiliated him. He was determined to get even with Crocker at the first opportunity. And then there was that greaseball Carlos Garieta; sooner or later Katy would blurt out to him what had happened. That meant he would have to kill the Spaniard. The problem was when...

When Katy and Crocker failed to show by noon of the next day, Christian gave way before the entreaties of his own cowpunchers and agreed to let them go and scour the range for a sign of the missing couple.

It was during the course of their search that the cowboys discovered that the homesteaders living on the CM land were packing their possessions and preparing to move north. When they brought the news back to Christian Barrett he almost choked over his supper.

'Moving...' he shouted. 'Moving to where?'

The cowpoke who'd brought him the news looked longingly at the bowl of broth set down in front of the rancher, but Christian didn't invite him to sit down.

'They're going to settle on Shallow Creek land,' the cowboy replied. 'Ma Kemp has

179

offered them a free lease if they'll help out with round-ups and branding from time to time.'

Christian Barrett pushed the plate away from him; he'd suddenly lost his appetite. That wily old Ma Kemp was replacing her lost cowhands by recruiting squatters who felt nothing but hatred for the CM outfit.

That meant that it was more important than ever to gain control over the Garieta ranch. He must find Rosita and bring her back at all costs. If Blayney hadn't vanished he must be killed so that Christian Barrett and Rosita could start again with a clean slate.

The second piece of news reached the ranch two hours later. A pair of cowboys had intercepted Carlos Garieta on his way to the CM ranch. Carlos had given them a message for his intended brother-in-law. Rosita Garieta and Ed Blayney were still in Chalmer's Hill. The next day Carlos was going into the township to kill Blayney.

If Christian wanted to come along Carlos

Garieta would wait for him at noon at the point on the trail known as Poplar Fork...

In the space of a few days Ed Blayney's life had been completely overturned. He'd left the CM ranch seemingly friendless and purposeless, yet now he found himself with the responsibility of a job, a woman of his own and two fugitives, Katy Barrett and Crocker, who were fleeing the wrath of a ruthless gunslinger, Jensen, and maybe his two cronies Pope and Young as well.

It was a warm afternoon even though evening was on the way and Blayney could feel the hot sun burning the back of his shirt as he strode up to the door of the jailhouse.

Marshal Staples rose sharply from his chair when his deputy entered.

'What's wrong?' Blayney inquired. 'You nervous or something?'

Staples nodded his head.

'I'm nervous,' he admitted. 'Christian Barrett and Carlos Garieta are in town and there's three hired guns with them that I've seen on wanted posters in more than one place.'

Blayney moved over to the window and looked out into the street. Chalmer's Hill wasn't a regular-shaped township. It had lots of sidestreets and alleyways where a gunman could hide and pick you off.

'Where are they?' he asked quietly.

'They were at the Blue Bear saloon last time I heard,' Staples told him. 'They were asking questions about where you and Rosita were staying. By the way, are the women safe?'

'Crocker's with them,' Blayney told him. 'He's well armed and he won't let anyone past him.'

He turned to face the lawman.

'I'd feel better if you went over there as well,' he said. 'Just in case.'

'Sure, I'll do that,' Staples assured him.

Blayney watched him put on his jacket. Staples wasn't wearing a gun; he never did, and he was too old to change his ways now.

'What are you going to do?' Staples asked him.

'I'm going to see what they want,' Blayney said.

As he spoke he began to unfasten the tin star on his shirt.

'I won't be needing this,' he told Staples.

'Why not?'

'I'm just a gunfighter like them,' Blayney explained. 'I won't hide behind a badge.'

Staples stomped around the table and confronted him.

'I thought you had more in you than that, Ed,' he said angrily. 'A group of killers are all set to ride roughshod over justice in this town, and all you see is a personal matter between you and them. Well, you go ahead and drop all your responsibilities and leave it to me to clear up the mess. And if I don't live that long let some other fool like me pick up that badge and try to figure out what to do next.'

Blayney averted his eyes under Staples' accusing stare.

'I only asked you to see that the women are alright.' he said. 'I don't want to get you involved in anything.'

'Well, I am involved,' Staples informed him sharply. 'I always was, and I always will be. That's something I guess a feller like you ain't never going to understand...'

Crocker heard the knock on the door and drew his Colt from its holster. He signalled to Rosita Garieta to get out of the firing line of the door.

'Who's there?' he called out.

The reply was muffled but the voice was recognizable.

'It's me, Carlos Garieta. I want to see my sister.'

Crocker turned to glance inquiringly at Rosita. The girl nodded her head.

'Are you alone?' Crocker asked.

'Yes, I'm alone,' Carlos assured him.

Crocker drew his Colt .45 as he opened the door a foot or so.

'You'd better be,' he said.

Carlos Garieta slid past him into the room. He didn't glance at Crocker or the gun Crocker had trained on him. Instead, he crossed the room stealthily, his eyes full of menace.

Rosita watched him approach, her head held high. Crocker tried to shout a warning to Carlos to keep away from the girl, but the atmosphere between brother and sister was electric and the words stuck in his throat.

Carlos glowered at the girl for a moment, then raised his hand in a smooth movement. As he prepared to whip the palm across Rosita's face she spoke up in a quiet but firm voice.

'Don't hit me,' she said. 'Or my husband will have to kill you!'

His hand hung in mid-air for a moment, then dropped loosely to his side. He was visibly deflated by his sister's words. Then the silence was broken.

'Carlos!'

He turned towards the inner door. Katy

Barrett was standing there, white-faced.

'Carlos,' she said, the tears running down her cheeks. 'Please forgive me...'

TWENTY ONE

The whiskey at the Blue Bear saloon helped Christian Barrett to relax as he waited for Carlos Garieta to come back. He wondered what would be the outcome if Carlos ran into Ed Blayney on his way to see his sister. One of the two was bound to die, and whichever it was would be good news for the CM spread.

Pope and Young were not drinking much but were amusing themselves playing dice for small stakes. They'd been in this sort of situation often in the past and were not unduly worried. Word had it that Blayney had been appointed deputy marshal of Chalmer's Hill, but he wouldn't be the first lawman they'd gunned down. Marshal Staples didn't even come into the reckoning; he was known as a talker, not a gunfighter.

Of the three of them it was Jensen who was the most ill-at-ease. He liked a clear-cut situation at all times, and at present the role of Carlos Garieta was bugging him. How long would it be before the Spaniard found out about his manhandling of Katy Barrett? Jensen didn't relish the idea of a knife in his back.

'The greaseball's been gone a long time,' he said suddenly, pulling himself up in his chair.

Christian glanced over at the saloon clock.

'Almost an hour,' he agreed. 'Something's kept him.'

Jensen sipped his drink moodily.

'D'you trust him?' he demanded.

Barrett pursed his lips.

'I need him to kill Blayney,' he replied.

'Any one of us can kill Blayney for you,' Jensen snorted.

'It's not the same,' Barrett pointed out.

'Rosita can't blame me if her own brother kills him.'

Jensen changed tack suddenly.

'Do you really want a greaseball like that marrying Katy?' he asked bluntly.

Christian smiled a cold smile.

'Who said anything about them marrying?' he said.

Jensen was encouraged by the reply. He had secret ambitions about Katy Barrett himself.

'It would be simpler if Carlos copped a bullet as well,' the gunslinger remarked slyly.

Christian nodded his head. This was as good a time as any to discuss the matter.

'It would have to look like an accident,' he said in an undertone.

'A lot of things can go wrong in a gunfight,' Jensen observed.

'That's right,' Christian agreed.

Outside the light was fading into evening. Christian Barrett got up and walked over to the counter.

'D'you keep a shotgun?' he inquired of the barman.

'Yessir.'

The rancher dropped a ten-dollar bill on the bar.

'I'll need a loan of it for a while,' he said. 'Me and my friends are going to take a stroll in town.'

Ed Blayney also noted the approach of evening. Normally at this time of day he did a rounding of the town, picking up rubbish where it had been thrown and generally tidying things up. It was an unsung and unglamorous side to a lawman's life but it was part of the duties and Marshal Staples insisted that their work should be done properly in all respects.

He deliberately chose a route that led through the sidestreets to the house Staples had loaned him. Crocker was there and maybe Staples was too, but he still needed to check on the girls' safety for his own peace of mind.

He had something else on his mind as well but he fought against admitting it to himself. Maybe this was the last time he'd see Rosita. Like most gunfighters Blayney was a realist, and he knew that the odds were badly stacked against him at present. Christian Barrett and the others were in town for a reason and he knew that that reason was him.

Maybe it was because he had so much on his mind that he failed to see the shadow projecting from the corner of a tumbledown shack on his left.

'Blayney...'

He froze as he heard Carlos Garieta's voice.

He could tell from the shadow where the Spaniard was standing. If that shadow made too swift a movement he knew he'd have to draw and shoot at random.

'They're gunning for you, Blayney,' Carlos informed him in little more than a whisper.

Blayney felt a shiver run up his spine.

'What about you, Carlos?' he asked.

Garieta gave a short laugh.

'I don't like what you did, Blayney, but I'll get over it. Did Katy tell you what Jensen tried to do to her?'

'She told Rosita,' Blayney replied.

'I'm going to kill Jensen,' Carlos said, moving out into the open.

Blayney looked at him. The Spaniard was wild-eyed.

'I don't think that's a good idea,' Blayney observed. 'Jensen's no pushover. It'd be better if you went back and helped Crocker to look after Katy and Rosita.'

'You're going up against Jensen, aren't you?' Carlos asked.

'Jensen's going up against me,' Blayney corrected him. 'Besides, Staples tells me I'm a deputy marshal and that I should act like one, so I ain't got much choice.'

'Leave Jensen to me,' Carlos insisted. 'He's mine.'

The young fool must have a death wish, Blayney thought. He tried one more time.

'You're angry, Carlos,' he said. 'You'll have

no chance if you're angry.'

Carlos nodded his head.

'I am angry,' he admitted. 'But when I meet Jensen I shall forget my anger.'

He turned quickly and disappeared into the gap between the two buildings. Blayney didn't attempt to call him back or even see where he was heading. From now on he'd have enough on his hands without worrying about Carlos Garieta's private vendetta.

When Christian and the three hired guns left the Blue Bear saloon, Jensen had already decided to split from the others and attend to his own business – Carlos Garieta. The bartender had given them clear directions as how to get to the house occupied by the new deputy marshal. Carlos had already set out for the place and now Jensen intended to trace his steps and kill him on his way back.

That would leave Pope and Young to take care of Ed Blayney. The marshal and deputy marshal would have to be seen by the townsfolk to be doing their duty, and that would keep them to the main thoroughfare or thereabouts. If anything happened he'd be bound to hear the shots and could hurry back to lend a hand if his fellow gunslingers couldn't handle the situation.

— As soon as Jensen crossed the main road and entered one of the sidestreets he had the uncomfortable feeling that he was being watched. With the canniness of a professional gunfighter he kept to the shadows and avoided the declining evening sunshine. Every few yards he stopped and looked around. There was nobody in sight, but still the feeling was there. He felt a light sweat break out on his forehead. The sooner he came face to face with someone the better.

Meanwhile Carlos Garieta tracked the gunslinger like a cat tracking a mouse. The difference was, he knew, that in this case the mouse was the more dangerous of the two. Also, Jensen's behaviour showed him to be aware of Garieta's presence. Carlos began to respect his enemy and as he did so his anger gave way to cold determination. He remembered Ed Blayney's warnings, not only the most recent but also what he'd said in the barn at the Garieta ranch. It struck him suddenly that he liked Ed Blayney and he hoped neither of them would die before he had the chance to tell him so.

There was no longer any doubt in the young Spaniard's mind. Jensen was on his way to Rosita's place. There was no longer any need to follow him. Much better to steal a march on him and intercept him along the way...

Jensen could make out a figure at the corner of the sidestreet ahead of him. As he approached cautiously the feller's head turned and he saw that it was Carlos Garieta.

Carlos instantly raised his finger to his lips to urge Jensen to approach silently. The gunslinger could have killed him then, but the signal and the open expression on Garieta's face indicated to him that the Spaniard's quarrel was still with Blayney and that even now he had the deputy marshal under surveillance.

Jensen knew that if he drew now he'd get Garieta but then he'd have to face Blayney without the comfort of backing from Pope and Young. Much better to join the Spaniard and pick Blayney off from there.

When he'd got to within ten yards of the corner, Carlos Garieta detached himself from the wall of the building without any attempt at concealment. Jensen smelled a rat at once. He'd already noted that Carlos wore his holster on his left hip and he kept a close eye on the Spaniard's dangling left hand. Jensen felt no doubt as to his ability to blow Garieta to hell.

'Katy has told me everything,' Carlos told him gravely. 'Now I kill you.'

'You do that,' Jensen encouraged him. Then he saw the flash of steel in Garieta's right hand.

Even as the gunslinger drew the knife was in flight. It pierced deep into Jensen's chest but still his gun levelled and began blazing.

Carlos remembered Blayney's words in the barn, and he threw himself sideways as he released the dagger. His action saved his life but didn't save him from injury. One of Jensen's slugs slammed into his shoulder and sent him spinning against the wall of the house.

The fire and pain blurred his vision but he had no doubt that the motionless figure in front of him was dead. The problem now was whether the shooting would bring Jensen's cronies looking for him. He retreated into one of the alleyways, leaving a trail of fresh blood in the dust as he went.

A few minutes later Marshal David Staples passed by, drawn by the sound of gunfire. He studied the body of Jensen where it lay with the knife protruding from the rib-cage. He didn't like violence in his town, didn't like it one bit.

He thought bitterly about the trouble-free years he'd enjoyed as marshal. Well it looked as if the honeymoon was over. He thought of Blayney as well; an hour earlier he'd talked him out of resigning as deputy marshal. Now Blayney was out there somewhere with killers stalking the streets.

Staples reached down and prised the Colt from the dead gunfighter's fingers. At least it would lend some credence to his authority, he thought, but at the same time he prayed that he wouldn't have to use it.

The sound of the fusillade of shots made Christian Barrett start. There was no sign of life on the main street, since the word had spread that there was likely to be a showdown before nightfall.

'What was that?' he asked anxiously of the two men at his side.

Pope managed to keep an impassive expression, though he felt distaste and contempt for the nervous rancher who'd acted so brave in the safety of the saloon.

'It sounds like Jensen,' he said calmly. 'D'you want me to go see what's going on?'

'No, you stay here with me, both of you!'

The two gunfighters could read the alarm

in Barrett's voice and it made them uneasy. They didn't know where they stood in this township and they knew they had to stay cool. The last thing they needed was for the young rancher to panic.

'We ain't going anywhere, Mr Barrett,' Young assured him like a nursemaid consoling a child. 'You just tell us what you want us to do, and we'll do it.'

'We ... we'll wait for Jensen to come back,' Christian said, trying to insert a note of authority into his voice.

'That's fine by me,' Pope replied, hardly disguising the scorn he felt.

Young's gaze was fixed on the far end of the street. A figure was walking towards them out of the sunset.

'Who's that for Chrissake...' Christian Barrett demanded. 'Jensen?'

Young shook his head.

'Nope,' he answered. 'It looks like the deputy marshal to me.'

Barrett's eyes narrowed into slits. He'd spotted an alleyway he could hide in and observe everything that went on from there.

'Then kill him,' he ordered them. 'Kill him!'

They didn't even notice him slipping away. Their minds were now set on the task ahead. It was a two-to-one situation and they felt comfortable. As they moved out into the street, keeping well apart in order to make it more difficult again for their opponent, they were pleased to see him making for the sidewalk. Blayney was obviously seeking a shaded spot but they judged it to be a mistake on his part since they no longer had to stare into the setting sun to see him.

Blayney figured things differently. So he'd had the sunlight at his back, but he'd been exposed out on the street and there was no way he could outgun two of them at the wide angle they'd presented him with. Their very caution showed their experience. He wasn't going to sell his life cheaply.

They waited for his next move, and were surprised when he stepped out of the shadow to address them.

'Where's Jensen?' he asked.

Pope watched the deputy marshal with unblinking eyes.

'You tell us, Blayney,' he replied.

'I got a message for him,' Blayney went on. 'I want to talk to him about Katy Barrett.'

Blayney could just about see Young from the corner of his eye. He had a shrewd suspicion how the two gunfighters would act; Pope was the nearest and therefore the least likely to draw first. Young would go for his gun and hope to catch Blayney in a quandary. Blayney took a step backwards into the shadow and the partial cover of a wooden roof-support, as Young drew his pistol dead on cue.

Blayney made his draw with his shoulder pressed tight against the wooden strut. His gun slid from his holster as Young's first slug smashed a window to the right of him. Pope's gun arm was also levelling at him but Blayney fired first and Pope's left leg gave under him.

Young fired again and the bullet struck the

edge of the pillar and ricocheted harmlessly onto the sidewalk. Still Blayney kept his eye on Pope. If the gunslinger had had the sense to lie still he'd have been safe; instead he raised his body on one elbow to take aim again. Blayney couldn't afford the luxury of being under siege on two fronts so he fired his second shot and took the top off Pope's head.

The street went quiet for a moment and Blayney wondered whether Young had used three shots or four. What was certain was that he'd have to seek cover before attempting to reload. If Blayney could move fast enough Young might waste another slug or two. It was that thought that brought the deputy marshal running out into the open street.

He heard a shot and decided it was time to turn. He half spun round and saw Young within easy range. At that very moment he spotted Marshal David Staples hobbling across the road as quickly as he could some thirty yards behind the gunslinger.

Blayney hesitated for a split second rather than hit Staples with a stray bullet. It almost proved fatal for him as Young's next shot struck the crown of his stetson and threw the hat flying yards behind him. Maybe Young's gun was empty but it wasn't a chance Blayney cared to take. He thumbed the hammer of his Colt savagely and threw two slugs into Young's body. The gunfighter keeled over clutching his stomach and lay there groaning for a moment or two, then he heaved a loud sigh and went still.

Staples hadn't crossed the thoroughfare in the middle of a gunfight for his health's sake. His action had brought him into the same sidestreet where Christian Barrett was concealed with the shotgun in his hands.

Barrett had seen the lame lawman approach but all his attention was focussed on the long shadow of Ed Blayney who was advancing slowly along the main street of Chalmer's Hill.

'It's all over, Christian,' Staples said quietly. 'Put the gun down on the ground.'

Barrett glanced round and thought how incongruous the old stage-driver looked with a gun in his hand. If it hadn't been for the fact that Blayney was only a few yards away the young rancher would have laughed out loud.

'Go grab yourself a drink, marshal,' he replied. 'Tell the barman it's on me.'

Staples kept the gun levelled at Christian's back for a few moments then let it fall wearily to his thigh.

'Blayney...' he called out in a last attempt to avert disaster. 'Don't come any closer.'

Christian Barrett saw the shadow freeze and he felt a cold anger in his gut. He spun the shotgun around and squeezed on the twin triggers.

When Blayney heard the shots he ran forward, his gun drawn. As he turned the corner he saw that the shotgun had torn a large hole in the planks of the sidewalk a few feet from where Marshal Staples was standing. Opposite, Christian Barrett was in a sitting position with his legs splayed apart, his eyes wide open and blood streaming down from a gaping wound in his throat. No seasoned gunman would have aimed for the neck; Staples had just got lucky, that was all.

The marshal didn't look too good so Blayney gave him something else to think about.

'Jensen's still around,' he said. 'I'm going to look for him.'

Staples looked at him if he was part of a dream he was having.

'Jensen's dead,' he said dully. 'I'll take you there.'

Blayney followed him across the main street which was still deserted apart from a few curious dogs who'd smelt blood.

Jensen's body was still in the alleyway, the knife protruding from its chest.

'There's a trail of blood,' Blayney said after a rapid examination of the ground. 'It looks like Carlos got hit as well.'

They turned into another alley and saw two figures coming towards them. Crocker was advancing slowly, a gun in one hand, his other arm supporting Carlos Garieta who was nursing his injured shoulder that was still bleeding inside his shirt.

The four men came face to face and for a moment none of them spoke; then Carlos Garieta managed to smile as he addressed Ed Blayney.

'What's wrong,' he asked. 'Haven't you seen blood before?'

'Sure I have,' Blayney replied. 'But not *sangre castiza*...'

The publishers hope that this book has given you enjoyable reading. Large Print Books are especially designed to be as easy to see and hold as possible. If you wish a complete list of our books please ask at your local library or write directly to:

Dales Large Print Books
Magna House, Long Preston,
Skipton, North Yorkshire.
BD23 4ND